Light Years: A Girlhood in Hawai'i

The Big Girls

I Myself Have Seen It: The Myth of Hawai'i

One Last Look

In the Cut

Sleeping Beauties

The Whiteness of Bones

My Old Sweetheart

The Life of Objects

The Life of Objects

SUSANNA MOORE

ALFRED A. KNOPF · NEW YORK · 2012

THIS IS A BORZOI BOOK
PUBLISHED BY ALFRED A. KNOPF

Library of Congress Cataloging-in-Publication Data

Moore, Susanna.
The life of objects / Susanna Moore.—1st ed.
p.   cm.
"This is a Borzoi book."
ISBN 978-0-307-26843-3
1. Germany—History—1933–1945—Fiction.   2. Self-realization in women—
Fiction.   3. Aristocracy (Social class)—Germany—Fiction.   I. Title.
PS3563.O667L54 2012
813'.54—dc23   2012019890

Jacket photograph by Hugo Erfurth © 2012 Artists Rights Society (ARS),
New York / VG Bild-Kunst, Bonn
Jacket design by Jason Booher

Manufactured in the United States of America

First Edition

To Richard Moore and Cheryl Hardwick,
and to Michael Moore

The Life of Objects

1938

My name is Beatrice Adelaide Palmer. I was born in 1921 in Ballycarra, County Mayo, the only child of Elizabeth Givens and Morris Palmer of Palmerstown. My family had come down in the world, and we were no longer gentry, but we weren't tenant farmers, either (not educated at university, but not peasants). I attended a small school kept by Mr. Hugh Knox, a Church of Ireland clergyman with a passion for birds who gave lessons in Latin grammar and mathematics. As there was no lending library in Ballycarra, Mr. Knox encouraged his pupils (there were only three of us) to read from his own collection of books—*Robinson Crusoe*, *Cranford*, Shakespeare, Dickens, Trollope and Thackeray, *Jane Eyre*, the sermons of Jonathan Swift, *Grimm's Fairy Tales*, George Eliot, Lewis Carroll, Thomas Hardy, *The Journal of the Beagle*, *The Complete Father Brown*, *The Crusade and Death of Richard I*, Siegfried Sassoon, *The Cloister and the Hearth*, *The Diary of Samuel Pepys*, and *Biggles and the Black Peril* (a book that instilled in me a terror of Russians).

Mr. Knox also had an extensive collection of bird journals and scientific papers, and although much to Mr. Knox's disappointment, I didn't read the ornithology books, I read the novels, some more than once, and the fairy tales many times (particularly the story of Little Red Riding Hood, who Dickens claimed was his first love: "I felt that if I could have married Little Red Riding Hood, I should have known perfect bliss"). When Mr. Knox went to Dublin each fall, he always returned with a book that he knew would give me pleasure, such as the new Daphne du Maurier or Agatha Christie, and to my delight he allowed me to keep those books. Mr. Knox liked to say that novels help to show us that the world is a place of strangeness, ruled by chance, which makes it difficult to maintain our certainties. I had no certainties other than my desire to leave Ballycarra.

Mr. Knox encouraged his students to accompany him on his excursions to study the birds of the Moy Estuary, but I was the only one who walked with him, just as I was the only one who read his books. That is when he taught me to fish, giving me the name of Maeve of Connacht, the pirate queen.

He was the sole companion of my girlhood. Were it not for Mr. Knox, my loneliness would have been more than I could bear. When he was not distracted by fieldwork, I asked him questions. Mr. Knox, unlike anyone in our village, had been in the world. He had, by his own admission, seen things. He'd been to university in England and had served in the Great War. He had even traveled in Canada before taking orders. I had been once to Glasgow as a small child with my mother and father. My mother was ashamed of her relatives and never spoke of the trip, other than to remind my father that he'd been sick crossing the Irish Sea.

I was a quiet girl, by all accounts, conversation considered an unnecessary luxury by my parents. I heard no family tales or instructive anecdotes, my head filled instead with the stories of willful heroines, vivacious of temperament unlike myself, with whom I shared a longing for the world and its imagined pleasures—irresistible girls like Eustachia Vye, Maggie Tulliver, Becky Sharpe, and even the wicked Gwendolen Harleth.

It is no wonder that my curiosity threatened my peace of mind. I couldn't explain my thoughts, or begin to understand them. There was nothing in my family that would have anticipated such a seeking temperament as I possessed, a mystery which often distressed me. Without knowing how to remedy it, I understood that I was already estranged from my parents, if only in my desires, and that my efforts to earn my mother's regard were fruitless. She behaved more like a stepmother to me than a mother, and now and then I questioned if I was indeed her child.

She rarely spoke about herself and I knew very little about her. She'd worked as a waitress in the teashop in Sligo where my father, a student at a nearby technical school, took his supper every Saturday night. When my grandfather Palmer died shortly after their marriage, my father abandoned his studies to take over the family shop. My mother said that she'd never have married him had she known she'd be lost for the rest of her miserable life in the filthy bogs of west Ireland. She claimed to envy her sisters—one had run off with a commercial traveler, and the other had drowned in childhood. She was born a fool, she said, and she would die a fool. I did not think her foolish—she had too little charm for that—but her disappointments had rendered her bitter and unkind. My father and I were in constant dread of her. I lived in a chaos of desire and disappointment.

When I turned fifteen, my mother, who had long felt that Mr. Knox was filling my head with ideas that would do me little good in the world of haberdashery, took me from school to work in the shop. I was heartbroken, but no amount of pleading or persuasion could make her change her mind. Mr. Knox sent word through one of my fellow pupils, a smirking boy named Peter whose father was bailiff at the castle, that he hoped I would continue to read his books and to accompany him on his walks. My mother told Peter to inform our teacher that I was far too busy to idle in the woods.

A few days later, I announced that Mr. Knox wished to

engage me to clean the schoolroom. My mother, who welcomed the chance for me to earn a little money, allowed me to go to the rectory every Saturday when the shop was closed. When I told Mr. Knox my lie, knowing that my mother would demand to see the money, he said that I'd more than earned it, having read aloud to him for years. He was happy to give me a shilling every week.

Mr. Knox particularly liked me to read from *The Peterborough Bestiary*, which I'd come to know by heart: *Cranes divide the night into sentry-duty and they make up the sequence of the watches by order of rank, holding little stones in their claws to ward off sleep. When there is danger they make a loud cry.* The bestiary also advised that parrots be beaten with an iron rod should they refuse to talk, a passage that always made him laugh. He had a pet gull named Wedgwood that he'd raised (from the shell, he liked to say), and the bird often accompanied us on our field trips. Mr. Knox also taught me to keep his lists in order, and through observing the comfort he took in them, I began to keep lists of my own. In my first list, made when I was twelve, I wrote: *A fine pair of shoes, a diary with a key, a parrot, a curling iron.*

Although we had few customers, my mother did not let me read in the shop, lest it appear that I gave myself airs. To ease the tedium, I studied my father's ledgers as if they held the answers to all that I longed to know. They were narrow books with maroon board covers, and in them were kept the names of customers and their transactions. I conceived elaborate tales to match each entry. The notation *Mrs. Dennis Gurney, doz.*

handkerchiefs, no monogram, one bolt pink tulle, three packets needles made me wonder what Mrs. Gurney possibly meant to do with so much tulle (as it was pink, it could not be for a bridal veil) and, less interesting, why she had chosen plain handkerchiefs, as the monogramming was done to order by my mother and free of charge. That the Catholic priest, Father Timothy, fancied costly cashmere hose that had to be ordered from Dublin was, thanks to my youth, less compelling, although mildly titillating.

There were only two boys in Ballycarra who were not Catholic (my former schoolmates), and my mother took care to remind me that if I did not soon make a match with one of them, I would end my days a spinster. I found the boys to be ignorant and dull, and I avoided them whenever I saw them in the village. I was intrigued by the handsome Catholic boys, despite (or thanks to) my father's horror of Roman Catholics. He'd been told by a great-aunt that the audience at a Punch and Judy show in Killala had cheered at the news that the French had landed nearby, and the shock of it had done it for him, even though the landing had been one hundred years before his birth. I was curious about the Catholic girls, too, but they kept themselves apart, a snub that infuriated my mother, who, despite her complaints, had done well for herself.

It didn't take long to exhaust the mysteries of the shop's ledgers, and I began to teach myself to crochet, copying the patterns I found in the ladies' magazines my father kept on behalf of his customers, studying them until the pages grew soft with use.

I stole lengths of thread from the shop, rolling them into a ball until I'd accumulated enough to make my first cuff (I unraveled it eight times before it was to my liking, and even then I didn't think it good enough). Copying Mr. Knox's notes had given me patience and an appreciation of tidy handiwork, and the hours I spent sewing seemed to pass in a dream. Silence had become natural to me, and a tendency to secrecy, if not dissimulation.

I sewed at night, using the ends of candles I found in the kitchen, which burned for an hour or two. My mother, naturally suspicious, took to creeping up the attic stairs to make sure that I was not committing any sins of impurity. At the sound of her footstep, despite her attempt at stealth, I hid my work under a blanket, my furtiveness undoubtedly encouraging her fantasies of vice. My mother was right to worry, as the patterns from Madeira and Brussels and Murano served to further excite my restlessness. I began to dream of the day when I would escape from Ballycarra.

I determined to teach myself to make lace after I saw a Youghal tablecloth drying on a hedge, said to have been made by the girls who sewed in the byre across the bridge, where the moist warmth of the cows kept their thread supple and their hands from stiffening in the cold. I wished to see more of their work, but my mother would not allow me to call on them. It confused me that girls considered so uncivilized could have made something as beautiful as the lace tablecloth with its design of ferns and heather. On warm evenings, I used to watch from the dark shop as the girls made their way to the river, and sometimes I wished that I were Roman Catholic, if only for the summer.

One morning, I brought down one of my finished pieces— a lace collar I'd studied in a magazine—and left it on the counter for my father to find when he opened the shop. Neither my mother nor my father mentioned it, but my father began to leave spools of thread at the foot of the stairs for me. By the end of the year, I had a dozen Valenciennes cuffs and collars, which I again left for my father to find. To my surprise, he offered to display my work in the window of the shop. Although the lace did not sell, even marked very low, it was admired, and I began to gain a certain small renown in the neighborhood. My father, who rarely praised me, reminded me that his father, my grandfather Palmer, had been notorious for the beauty of his salmon flies and suggested that I had, perhaps, inherited something after all.

A few days after my seventeenth birthday, a woman in a rabbit coat stepped into the shop during a sudden rainstorm and noticed me sewing in a corner. My father, who recognized Lady Vaughan, pulled out the tray that held my finished pieces (my mother was not there) and, while he shook out her umbrella, encouraged her to look at them. A week later, a package was delivered to the shop marked with my name, causing my mother to fear that an embarrassing mistake had been made. Inside the parcel were two books of lace patterns, a gift from

Lady Vaughan to me. Not long after, Lady Vaughan's maid came into the shop to order half a dozen pieces of bed lace for her ladyship, so infuriating my mother that she did not speak to me for the rest of the week, and only then to tell me that Mr. Knox had sent me a box of books, which she had returned.

My bed lace so pleased Lady Vaughan that she asked if I would make her a black lace shawl in time for a hunt ball in September. With my father's permission, I no longer waited on customers but sewed in the back room where the light was best, and by summer's end, my fingers were so red and swollen that I had to soak them each night in hot water and salt. I was afraid that my work would not be fine enough and that Lady Vaughan would be disappointed, but despite my fear, I also felt a strange elation, so new to me that I often laughed out loud, causing my mother to leave the room. When Lady Vaughan's maid came to collect the finished shawl, I made her an awkward curtsy and rushed into the yard, where I sat for an hour to compose myself. That evening, Lady Vaughan sent a note thanking me for my "lovely" work, enclosing two one-pound notes with an order for two collars and six cuffs.

The morning after the ball, it was known throughout the village that a guest at the castle, a foreign lady in Ireland for the hunting, had noticed my shawl and had asked Lady Vaughan where she had come by such exquisite lace. The lady, who was said to be a cousin of the Tsar, wore a long white taffeta skirt and black sweater to the ball, with a necklace of turquoise and diamonds, a costume so outlandish that by breakfast it had been described to my mother with screams of laughter by our neighbor, Mrs. Greeley, a maid at the castle (kind Lady Vaughan had worn claret velvet and her garnets). My mother announced that the lady was no more a Russian princess than she was, but I listened with fascination. There had never been a moment when I did not long for the world beyond Bally-carra, and to be offered a glimpse of it by a princess who wore a wooly to a ball was more than I'd imagined possible.

The foreigner—there was no mistaking it was she—came to the shop the following day. I was embarrassed when my mother, who was knitting in a chair, did not rise to greet her, and I rushed to bring a chair from the kitchen. When I returned, my mother ordered me from the shop.

To my confusion, the lady followed me into the street, catching up with me to ask if I'd care to walk by the river—the salmon were running, and she liked to watch the men casting, drops of water flying from their lines, she said, like jewels. Her name was Countess Hartenfels (although she spoke English with a foreign accent and she certainly looked like she could be a relation of the Tsar, she was not, to my relief, Russian). She said that she'd come to the shop in search of "that magician Miss Palmer," and she confessed her surprise at discovering I was a girl, having expected an elderly gentlewoman in mittens.

Linking her arm in mine (something that no grown woman had ever done, including my mother), she said that she'd like to see more of my lace. She admitted that she herself did not wear lace, except as *lingerie*. I'd never heard the word spoken, although I'd read it in magazines, pronouncing it with a hard *g*, and I didn't understand her at first. She admired lace on oth-

ers, however, particularly on her dear friend Dorothea Metzenburg, who lived in Berlin and owned a rare and extremely
valuable collection of lace. The countess was on her way to
Germany to visit the Metzenburgs. "You'd find them sympathetic," she said confidingly. "Felix has the best manners
in Europe." The intimacy of her tone, as well as her physical
nearness, made me tremble with happiness. She spoke as if I
understood everything that she said and, even more flattering,
all that she did not say. When we returned to the village, having walked as far as the Ridge Pool, I stole into the house to
gather my lace to show her, proudly spreading my work along
the damp stone rampart of the bridge.

Countess Hartenfels met me again the next afternoon. People
stared at us as we passed, and in my excitement, I told her
the names of the birds that I spotted along the river (a goo-
sander and the rare killdeer), aware that the creature in black
riding habit and veiled top hat, strolling with her arm linked
in mine, was, at least in Ballycarra, rarer than any killdeer. The
countess, who seemed a bit distracted, a quality that I took
for sophistication, said that she, too, was *quite* fond of birds,
even if she knew nothing about them. Her way of speaking,
in which she exaggerated unexpected words, was confusing to
me. I wasn't accustomed to emphasis, and I gave significance
to certain of her words and phrases that she perhaps didn't
intend. When she claimed *never* to have seen lace such as mine,
I believed her.

Shortly before the countess was to leave Ballycarra, she suggested that I accompany her to Berlin. I would live in the household of her friends, the Metzenburgs, where I would make lace. If I found myself unhappy, a condition she considered unlikely, I could, of course, return to Ireland. Convinced that she was mocking me, I paid her no mind, but she persisted, describing the amiability of her friends, the Metzenburgs, to whom she was devoted, and the excitement of the great city, until I could think of nothing else, causing my mother to ask if I were ill. I said nothing to her of the countess's invitation but called on Mr. Knox to ask his advice.

As we walked in the water meadow where he'd first taught me to fish, he saw a short-toed lark and stopped to note it in his journal. I told him, somewhat boastfully, of my unlikely acquaintance with the countess and of the extraordinary proposal she had made me. To my disappointment, he said nothing, only asked if I agreed that there had been fewer corncrakes that year. When I again mentioned the countess, he hushed me, not wishing to startle a redwing that we were following to its nest in an elm. It was my job to carry the long pole that we used to steal nests, and in my distraction, I caught the net in some brambles, causing him to glance at me with uncustomary impatience.

On the way home, he was unusually silent. I knew that he would eventually tell me his mind—I only had to be patient. He motioned to me to wait as he lit his pipe, then put away his matchbox, and we continued across the field. He wished to check the duck decoys that he kept in the mere, as they attracted large colonies of gadwall and grebe each fall (a deception that always left me melancholy). As we walked, he said that men who had reason to know were fearful that a war with Germany was coming, and he hoped that I was giving the countess's invitation some thought. Despite Mr. Knox's attempts to educate me, all of my history came from novels—I knew nothing of a coming war. Even if such a war were imminent, I did not see how it could affect me. I was the citizen of a free state.

He tapped his pipe on the heel of his boot and ground the embers into the dirt. "Who will read to me?" he asked.

I said that it was thanks to him, to his teaching and to the books that he had encouraged, even pressed me to read, that I had such a yearning for the world and that surely he, of all people, would not deny me the chance to indulge it. I said that it was unlikely that I would ever have such an opportunity again. He agreed somewhat wryly, and I realized from his tone that he would forgive me for leaving him. When we reached the rectory, he gave me his blessing and kissed me on the head. I promised that I would write to him.

The following morning, I announced to my parents that I was leaving Ballycarra to sew lace for a family in Berlin. My mother promptly declared that I was suffering one of my attacks of grandeur and refused to believe me, even after I asked my bewildered father to loan me a cardboard suitcase from the store's stock. I told them that the countess, who was arranging for my passport (Lord Vaughan's brother was in Dublin Castle), would meet me at the train station in two days' time.

The night before I left, as I packed and packed again my few belongings (my books of lace), my father came up the stairs to the attic. "I don't know where you come by it," he said, sitting at the end of my bed. "Your mother says it was the books that did it." He could not bring himself to look at me. He'd made me a present of a new pair of brogues, and I was having trouble fitting them into the small case.

I stopped my fussing. "The books saved me," I said. "And the lace."

I sat next to him on the bed and took his hand. I was not accustomed to touching him, and I was embarrassed—I could smell turf smoke on his jacket, and there was a trace of ash on his shirt. "I haven't much to give you," he said, tucking a pound into my pocket. "Nothing to get you out of trouble when it comes. Your mother will never forgive you."

"Think of it as an apprenticeship, Father. I'm going out to work."

"I have a sinking feeling that woman's a Papist," he said with a sigh. He rose stiffly and made his way cautiously down the narrow stairs, his head level with the floor when he stopped to say good night.

My mother would not walk with us to the station in the morning, but Mr. Knox was waiting on the platform with a book for me, *The Ornithology of Shakespeare*, which he'd inscribed *To Maeve, in the hope that she will learn to fly, September 1938*. My father, suddenly tearful, kissed me on the cheek (he nodded shakily to the countess, and she gave him a chilly smile), handing me a letter as I boarded the train.

When I showed the countess Mr. Knox's present, she asked why my old schoolmaster had inscribed it to someone named Maeve. "I am Maeve," I said. "That's my real name." The countess looked puzzled, although not sufficiently interested to question me further. She opened a magazine and, somewhat to my relief, soon fell asleep.

I watched from the window as the familiar river slipped past, low and dark behind the rowan trees. My initial excitement had begun to fade, particularly after saying good-bye to Mr. Knox, and I had a stomachache. I was traveling to a strange country whose language I did not speak, with a strange woman whom I had known for eight days, to work for people whom I did not know at all. I wondered what in the world I'd been thinking (I knew exactly what I'd been thinking).

When I could no longer see the river, I read the letter that my father had slipped into my hand. My mother wrote that as I had left *the bosom of your loving family for foreign shores,* she hoped that my new friends would be willing to provide the home that I had so eagerly forsaken, as she no longer felt obliged to do so. I folded the letter and looked for a place to put it—I had no handbag, and I tucked it into Mr. Knox's book. My mother's coldness, although familiar to me, caused me pain, and I was grateful that the countess was not awake to see me cry.

Over the five days of our journey to Berlin, my misgivings began to disappear. Countess Hartenfels (who more and more reminded me of Trollope's Madame Goesler, tall, dark, and thin, and adept with her eyes in a way unknown to any Englishwoman) explained that her maid was in Munich awaiting her arrival, and asked if I would be able to assist her with her hair and clothes, a request that thrilled me. When I noticed her staring at me (it was then that I realized she could not be embarrassed), she said that while my hair was a bit thin, it was not a bad shade of brown. And, *gracias a Dios,* I was not a redhead.

I had my own berth on the train from Calais, meeting Countess Hartenfels for meals in the dining car or in her private compartment, where I helped her to dress (pinning, fastening, combing, admiring). Her elegance left me feeling both threadbare and inspired, and by the time that we reached Belgium, I'd vowed to model my personal habits on those of the countess, even if my scant means (I had nothing) would be something of a constraint. At home, I wore my best dress to church and to the rare wedding or funeral. I wore tweed skirts and cardigans in the shop, with wool stockings and brogues. In summer, a cotton dress with lisle stockings and brogues. I had two flannel nightdresses, a shawl, a brown tweed coat, knit gloves, and a gray felt cloche that I wore to church. Rubber boots, of course. I did not own a party frock or a pair of high-heeled shoes. The countess dressed as if she were going to a party every day, wearing a suit (*tailleur,* she said, not "suit"), silk stockings, hat, and gloves. In the evening, she wore a chiffon tea gown, with satin shoes in shades of pale blue, gray, or rose. She carried a little gold bag in which she kept a compact, a lipstick, a lighter, and a cigarette case. She wore jewelry in the day (diamonds only after dark) and lipstick all of the time, even when she went to bed.

One night when she went to the dining car, leaving me to put away her clothes, I opened her red leather traveling case to dot some perfume—it was called *Cuir de Russie* and smelled like oranges and birch bark—behind my ears and on my wrists, and to brush some powder on my cheeks. I had just settled a black grosgrain hat on my head, tilting it so that the feather swept the side of my face as I had seen her do, when the door of the compartment opened. Startled, I knocked the box of powder to the floor.

She stood in the doorway, not particularly surprised at the sight of me in her hat (if I'd known any better, I'd have seen that she glinted). She came inside and closed the door, stepping around the spilled powder so as not to dirty her pretty shoes. "That color is a bit pale for you," she said. "Your skin is too yellow." I lifted the hat carefully from my head and put it in its box. I returned the empty box of powder and the scent bottle to her case. As she found the gold lighter she'd forgotten, she said, "They have Saint-Vaást oysters tonight." She opened the door and looked at me over her shoulder. "Are you coming?" I said that I'd be there in a moment, after I cleaned the powder from the floor.

As we crossed the German border, the countess, wearing a black silk peignoir (another new word for me, and one with unsettling connotations), suggested that she hold my passport for the rest of the journey, not wishing me to be further troubled by tiresome customs officers. Later, I threw my coat over my nightdress and made my way through the train to retrieve a book of lace I'd left in her compartment. As I moved from car to car, I felt that I had never been so happy in my life. My new independence, and my equally false sense that I could look after myself—the elation at having left Ballycarra behind—

were so strong that I even walked differently (the countess's own walk may have contributed to this). When I reached her door, I was surprised to hear laughter and a man's voice. I hurried back to my berth, my coat clutched around me, no longer quite so elated. I wondered if the countess had changed compartments and forgotten to tell me.

On the last night of our journey, as the countess smoked a cigarette after dinner in the dining car, she confided that she owed everything in the world to Herr Metzenburg. He'd taken her, Inéz Cabral, a young girl of fifteen, straight from Cuba, where he'd found her, and groomed and dressed her. Herr Metzenburg's house was the meeting place for the most fascinating men and women in Europe—not only politicians and diplomats, but writers and musicians and film stars—and he'd introduced her to a world that would otherwise have been closed, if not unknown to her. She confessed that her new manners and all the couture in Paris would not have amounted to anything in the end had Herr Metzenburg not stood behind her—and even then, she added mysteriously, there had been difficulties. After an arrangement of several years (living contentedly, she said, as slave and master), Felix invited his friend Count Hartenfels to a week's house party to introduce him to her. Three months later, she and the count were married in the private chapel of the Hartenfels castle near Munich. Felix, she said, showed his customary good taste by choosing not to give her away in marriage.

As my experience of arrangements was limited to the feeding of Mr. Knox's gull when he was in Dublin, I was understandably confused. I'd learned during my brief time with the countess, however, not to ask too many questions. She was a character in a fairy tale—Cinderella's fairy godmother, or the Snow Queen, perhaps—and I, who'd been properly bewitched, was accompanying her to a distant kingdom where I would live in an enchanted forest and spin flax into gold.

We arrived in Berlin in the late afternoon, traveling directly to the Metzenburgs' house on Fasanenstrasse. I thought at first that it was a hotel, but the countess said sharply that she had never stayed in a hotel in her life. She seemed puzzled when no one came to the door, and even more puzzled when Herr Metzenburg opened the door himself.

I could see that Herr Metzenburg must have forgotten that Countess Hartenfels was coming to stay. He kissed her hand with an amused, slightly mocking smile and led us to a pink drawing room, the look of surprise already disappearing from his face. I'd read about such things, of course, but I had it wrong—the man does not actually *kiss* the woman's hand but takes her hand in his own and, with a little bow, lowers his face to her fingers. The countess introduced me, explaining that I was a present for the Metzenburgs, which startled me. "You must allow me these little *cadeaux*," I heard her say as she took a cigarette from his case.

Herr Metzenburg may have forgotten that Countess Inéz

was coming to stay, but I was clearly a surprise. He turned to me smoothly, however, and said that he hoped that my journey had not been unnecessarily stressful, even if I was entering Germany, rather than leaving it, which tended to be more troublesome. Although Herr Metzenburg walked with a slight limp, he had a confident and easy way about him. I was so tongue-tied that I could only nod.

Behind him, a fair-haired, slender woman who could only be Dorothea Metzenburg floated noiselessly into the room, followed by an old man with a mustache and one eye, wearing white gloves and an apron, who immediately disappeared. Delicate and distracted, Frau Metzenburg did not have much to say, although she, too, seemed surprised to see us. Herr Metzenburg said something to her that I couldn't hear, but I thought I heard her say, "Ah, my very own lace maker."

The old man, without the apron but with a black monocle over his empty eye socket, returned with a tray of tea and cakes and dropped it onto a low mother-of-pearl table with a grunt. My idea of elegant manners had been taken from books and ladies' magazines, and I was surprised, especially when Herr Metzenburg waved away the fretful old man to pour the tea himself.

The countess had told me that after university in Heidelberg, Herr Metzenburg had been sent abroad by the German ministry as ambassador, first to London and then to Madrid. She also said that his grandfather had built all of the railroads in South America. "While it's not the most ancient of fortunes, it's perfectly lovely. He was so attractive that money *hardly* mattered. Madame de la Roche once slid over a small cliff for love of him." Although I was disappointed to discover that the Metzenburgs were not royal (and their house, although grand, was not a palace), both the excessive luxury and the excessive simplicity of the rooms, so unlike the dark and fussy rooms I'd conjured from magazines and books, made me wonder about all of the other things I'd imagined over the years. I'd always understood that if I were ever to have the things that I desired I would have to leave Ballycarra—I just hadn't known how much there was to desire.

As the old man showed us to our rooms (I heard Frau Metzenburg tell him to put me in a guest bedroom as the servants' rooms were filled with packing crates), the countess whispered that everything in my room was mine to use—bath towels, writing paper, soap, even the hot water (the last a bit unkind, I thought)—but it was an hour before I dared even pour myself a glass of water. The old man had made no mention of dinner, and by seven o'clock, I was hungry, despite the tea cakes. I heard footsteps in the passage and the sound of a bell, but no one came to my room, and I wondered if they'd forgotten me. Fortunately, a tin on a table next to the bed contained ginger biscuits, and I ate a few, then a few more, until the biscuits, to my dismay, were gone—it wasn't that I was still hungry, although I was, that worried me, but the fear that I shouldn't have eaten all of them. I fell asleep on top of the covers, my feet in a pair of silk slippers I found in the closet, waking in the middle of the night when I grew cold. I thought at first that I was in my own bed until the light from the streetlamp in

Fasanenstrasse, shining through the open curtains (I'd been unsure about closing them), reminded me that I was far from home.

The next morning, I had already bathed and dressed, made the bed (twice), and folded and refolded my towel and face-cloth when the old man, whose name was Kreck, came to my room to tell me that Herr Metzenburg wished to see me in the library. I followed him downstairs, certain that I was to be sent home. What most distressed me—even more than the thought of my mother's triumph—was the loss of my new bed with its silk sheets and satin quilt (and, yes, the hot water).

Herr Metzenburg appeared upset, looking for a moment as if he didn't remember me or why he wished to see me, before pointing to a chair and wishing me good morning. I thought at first that we could not possibly be in a library—red lacquer cabinets lined the walls, tall china pagodas between them— but then I noticed the books; there were hundreds of them.

There was the unfamiliar smell of coffee. A tray on the desk held two cups and saucers and a silver pot with an ivory han-dle. I was very hungry, and I glanced at the tray to see if there might be a scone or a piece of fruit, but there was nothing. Without asking if I wanted coffee, Herr Metzenburg made a sign to Kreck to pour me a cup.

When I felt that it was safe to look at him, the cup and saucer rattling in my hands (I wasn't used to drinking coffee, and I was nervous), I saw that he was staring out the window. There was a crowd in the street, running back and forth and shouting, and he asked Kreck to close the shutters. Like many people who command your attention, his head was a bit large for his body.

He wore his dark hair combed back from his face. His gray eyes reflected light in a way that made me uneasy—I felt that to look directly into his eyes was to risk revealing my most secret thoughts, had I any. He was close in age to my father. They were both about forty years old, but my father looked much older.

He turned to me and said that I was welcome to accompany him and Frau Metzenburg when they moved to their estate thirty miles south of Berlin. He said that a few days before my arrival he'd been offered his old position as ambassador in Madrid, which he had resigned in 1933, but he had refused the post, angering the foreign minister, who had immediately requisitioned the Metzenburgs' house (my pretty room!) and conscripted all of the servants under the age of fifty. He and Frau Metzenburg had been given ten days to empty the house. A circumstance of which the countess had perhaps been unaware when she left Ireland.

Although I was free to leave (he would, of course, arrange my passage), he had, upon thinking about it, realized that I might be of help to them in the weeks to come, especially as there were no longer any servants other than Kreck and the cook. He could offer me in return a small salary. He apologized that, given the events of the last few days, he could not warrant his protection, as it clearly amounted to very little. He feared that it was only a matter of time before there was a war between Germany, France, and England.

As I listened to him, I kept thinking that I had missed something. Something I couldn't see. I looked at the old man, but he was absorbed in arranging the silver on the tray. It was only when he signaled with an impatient shake of his head that I was keeping Herr Metzenburg that I was able to give him my answer.

Over the next few days, I noticed that people came to the house at all hours, even through the night. I thought at first that someone was ill—Kreck labored ceaselessly up and down the stairs, cursing under his breath as he carried trays of coffee and brandy, and newspapers and telegrams. Among the visitors were grave-looking men in uniform, dispatch cases under their arms. There were men in fur hats and dark coats, and I wondered if they might be Jews. I'd never seen a Jew, and I felt both excited and afraid.

Countess Inéz stayed for two nights, breaking her journey as she advised me to do when I traveled. On the day that she was leaving, I heard her ask Herr Metzenburg how anyone could possibly stay in one place for more than a month, and Herr Felix said, "Fortunately for you, a war is coming." The countess laughed and said that she was eager to return to Munich as she intended to divorce the count in order to marry a young Egyptian prince she'd met in Ireland.

Herr Felix said nothing, only lit a cigarette—he may have frowned; it was difficult to tell—but I was shocked. The idea of divorce was disturbing enough, but the countess had led me to believe that she trusted me. Despite her many confidences, she had clearly forgotten to mention the Egyptian prince. I consoled myself with the thought that she would certainly have told me in time—it was so busy in the house with the packing of the Metzenburgs' belongings and the coming and going of visitors that she clearly hadn't found the right moment to tell me. As she said good-bye, a swirl of chinchilla and gardenia, she kissed me on both cheeks. I was unused to kissing and made the mistake of touching her cheek with my lips, nearly tearing her veil.

"You'll be happy at Löwendorf, *niña*," she said, settling her veil. "And don't forget, Dorothea is inclined to *couche tôt*, but you will find Felix an excellent confidant." When I looked at her in surprise, she said, "Don't tell me I've misjudged you." Before I could ask what she meant, she was gone.

I felt a sudden panic at her leaving. It was easy to feel assured when she ceaselessly flattered and praised me. I'd been aware that all through our journey she'd been training me ("Not that spoon, my dear. And it's not necessary to stand when the porter enters . . ."), but with her departure, I would be on my own, when I would inevitably disappoint the Metzenburgs. I felt sick (what could *couche tôt* possibly mean?), but the thought of returning to Ireland was so much worse that I determined to make myself indispensable, at least until I'd been caught out and sent home, which would surely be only a matter of time.

My first task was to pack Herr Metzenburg's collection of turned ivory. Kreck proudly explained that turning ivory had once been the occupation of princes—"the tusks spun on the lathe in three directions at once!"—and I was terrified that I would break one of the delicate towers. Some of the pieces, thirty inches high but only five inches wide, had their own ebony cases, which made them easier to pack. When Kreck said that Herr Felix had begun collecting art while he was at school, eventually possessing one of the best collections in Europe, my dread increased, causing me to work with unaccustomed slowness.

That evening, I took a sheet of Frau Metzenburg's gray writing paper to my room, running my fingers over the little gold telephone and numbers at the top of the page, before hiding it in Mr. Knox's book.

Frau Metzenburg came into the pantry where Kreck and I were sliding soupspoons into little flannel bags to say that we would soon be at Löwendorf, where she had been born. I would have my own sewing room with a table and good light, and there would be people in the village to help Kreck. As she turned to leave, she asked if I would like to see the collection of lace she'd inherited from her father, who had died three years earlier. It was going to the bank at the end of the week, and she didn't know, given the state of things, when there'd be a chance to see it again. I was relieved to have an excuse to put aside my work for a moment, and I followed her up the stairs to the second floor.

The lace room (next to the gray-and-gold room that Kreck said was her private sitting room) had three chairs and a long table with brass apothecary lamps. A tray held several pairs of white cotton gloves and a magnifying glass. There were two long books, not unlike my father's ledgers, although Frau Metzenburg's were bound in red damask. Narrow drawers were built into the walls from floor to ceiling. A library ladder leaned against one wall. She turned on the lamps and handed me a pair of gloves.

I knew that I was staring, but I couldn't help myself. She was about thirty years old, younger than the countess and just as lovely, although there was something boyish about her, and secretive. She wore a navy-blue suit with two gold clips in the shape of question marks, a white crepe shirt with a narrow collar, and navy spectator pumps. Her lipstick was bright red. Her hair, the color of wet straw, was parted in the middle and twisted into a flat roll at the back of her neck. She was as weightless as a ghost.

"You didn't go to Mass with Inéz," she said, wiggling her fingers deeper into the gloves.

I was too surprised to speak.

"Even if you're not religious, you can believe in grace." She was so odd, so unlike anyone, even the characters in the books I'd read, that she made me uneasy. To make matters even stranger, she said, "But then I suspect that your moment of grace is yet to come." Then she asked where I would like to begin. It took me a moment to understand what she meant.

I pointed in front of me, and she slid a drawer from the wall and carried it to the table. Inside the drawer, on black velvet, were the yellowed hem of an alb sewn in *point de France*, a narrow panel of *point de Venise*, its delicate black dots sewn in a pattern of birds in flight, and a cravat of lace bees in what appeared to be mixed bobbin-and-needle lace. When I'd had my fill, I nodded, and she replaced the drawer with another.

"These are only fragments, of course," she said, not troubling to conceal a yawn. "The larger pieces—wedding dresses and altar cloths—have already been sent to the bank."

There were designs of windmills, stags, pyramids, cherubs, the Eiffel Tower, sailing ships, and double-headed eagles. There was simple Irish crochet work. She pointed with a gloved finger to a stiff linen ruff. "Sixteenth century. I think." She opened one of the books and found the description of the ruff, reading it to herself.

I again heard the sound of a bell, rung, I'd learned, to remind the Metzenburgs and their guests that it was time to dress for dinner. She pulled off her gloves and dropped them on the table (inside out, I noticed). "You have no interest in the women who made the lace," she said. "The blinding headaches and the torn fingers. It's the trousseau of the Dauphine that intrigues you. The handkerchief of the queen."

Had I not been so overwhelmed, I would have told her that I wasn't interested in the history of lace or even its romance. When I first taught myself to sew, it was the discovery that I could make Ballycarra disappear that had compelled me. More than that, I could make myself disappear. But as I no longer wished to disappear, I said nothing.

On my way to the servants' dining room at night, I sometimes passed a sour-faced, elderly woman, half squirrel, half bird, in an old-fashioned long black dress, carrying a tray with a plate of steamed fish, boiled potatoes with parsley, and beetroot. I sometimes saw her on the back stairs, a sweep of glittering evening gown draped across her two outstretched arms or carrying a tray of opera gloves, but when I tried to catch her eye, she refused to look at me.

When I asked Kreck about her, he grinned maliciously, the tips of his dyed black mustache nearly reaching his ears, and said that she was Frau Metzenburg's maid, Fräulein Roeder, who did not eat with the rest of the household. He'd been quick to add that although Fräulein Roeder's food was prepared for her especially, he and I ate the same food as the Metzenburgs. My mother, who'd worked as a young bride in a big house near Ballina, often complained of the indignities suffered by servants, particularly in regard to food, and I'd been happy to hear this from Kreck.

We met each evening for dinner at six o'clock, sitting across from each other as we ate the delicious food. He often seemed preoccupied, even distressed. I thought that a little conversation might cheer him, but when I attempted it, he did not bother to answer me.

I tasted for the first time that week an avocado pear and a pineapple, which I later sketched from memory to send to Mr. Knox, along with drawings of the birds I saw in the Metzenburgs' garden. I seldom thought of my mother and father, although I wrote to them (describing the food). I missed my old schoolmaster more than I missed my parents.

Because it was assumed that I would not break anything, given the deftness of my fingers, I was asked to wrap the Metzenburgs' collection of porcelain and pack it in crates of bran—that there were no other servants, except Kreck, who had a tremor, and the equally aged cook, Frau Schmidt (Fräulein Roeder, it was made clear, only attended to Frau Metzenburg), may also have been a consideration.

"Herr Felix beseeches your pardon," Kreck said in his stilted English, "as this will not be your accustomed duty, but when you are finished with the Nymphenburg, there is the Augsburg silver. And the Vincennes."

As I wrapped the porcelain in newspaper before settling it in the bran, my fingers grew black with newsprint, and I had to wash my hands frequently. As I went back and forth to the pantry, I lingered in the rooms, looking at all of the treasure that had accumulated over the years. The objects seemed more real to me than the people. I'd never seen anything as pretty as the silver plates decorated with bees, snails, and mulberries that had been bought, Kreck said, at the Duchess of Portland's auction. The dinner service with mythological figures in red and gold had been used by Frederick the Great at Sanssouci. A fluted white beaker and saucer, painted with plump Japanese children, had come from the palace in Dresden. Kreck, who seemed to know a great deal about the objects, had his own opinions. He thought the Duchess of Portland's silver plates *too* beautiful, causing me to question my own taste.

As I helped to fold a pair of velvet curtains, appliquéd with green monkeys, that had been hanging in Herr Metzenburg's bedroom—Kreck moved stiffly, due to his age and to palsy, turning the act of folding into a curious dance—I began to understand what the countess had meant when she said that

Herr Felix had a weakness for the playful, a gift she attributed to his instinctive *cocasserie* (which at first I took to mean "coquetry"). His bed linen and towels were embroidered, she said, with a silhouette of his pet donkey, Zara. The floor of the summer dining room was covered with fragrant apple matting. Plaster owls with yellow glass eyes blinked from the red lacquer cases in the library. The peonies in the pink drawing room were in tall blue-and-white vases ringed with what looked like the bars of a cage. Meissen, said Kreck when he saw me looking at them, but I didn't understand him.

Herr Metzenburg watched while we packed the carved panels of saints and a tiny velvet bed with silver Gothic spires, embroidered with seed pearls and emeralds. A bed for the Christ Child, Kreck said. I'd asked him if the Metzenburgs were Roman Catholic, but he hadn't answered me.

Several pieces were too large to manage on our own, and Herr Metzenburg hired porters from an auction house to help us. He watched apprehensively as the men moved a melancholy barefoot Christ, the size of a child, sitting on the back of an equally downcast donkey. It was called a *Palmesel*—there is no word for it in English, he said—and it depicted Christ's entry into Jerusalem on Palm Sunday. His expression as he watched the men pull it across the room—it sat on a wooden platform with four small wheels—was both rapt and anxious, his hand reaching to steady it. "The donkey would have had a leather bridle, which Our Lord held in his right hand." He said that almost all *Palmesel* had been made in the fifteenth century by local craftsmen. "Do you see how subtle it is, despite its apparent crudeness? The plump, perhaps even overfed donkey, Christ's scarred hands, the cracked hooves?" A special packing crate had been built to carry the statue, but it was too large to bring into the house. Herr Metzenburg led the procession as we solemnly escorted Christ and the donkey to the street where their crate awaited them. "There is a *Palmesel* in Verona I've been trying to get my hands on for years," Herr Metzenburg said with a smile. "It is said to contain the bones of the donkey that Christ rode into Jerusalem."

With the gradual disappearance each day of the Metzenburgs' belongings, the rooms grew larger and the ceilings higher. Although my experience of valuable objects had been limited to commemorative pickle forks (our dinner plates at home were called delft), I believed Kreck when he said that Herr Felix's taste was *vorzügliche.* Exquisite. My first German word.

One afternoon, I slipped a small silver dish into the pocket of my apron and a pen and an amber cigarette holder that Frau Metzenburg had left in an ashtray, and later I arranged them on a table in my room as if they were my own. I threw away my old Ballycarra list and made a new one. I wanted a navy wool coat with a gray fox collar, a good haircut, a silver brush and comb engraved with the letter *M* (for "Maeve"), and a few of what Kreck called *einige schöne Dinge*—perhaps a blue enamel desk set to match the pen, and an ivory sewing box.

I now and then caught sight of Frau Metzenburg as she glided from room to room, repeating her husband's lengthy and precise orders as she cajoled the hired men and calmed Kreck's nerves. If she bothered to acknowledge me, I blushed.

As there was no one left to do errands and Herr Metzenburg no longer wanted delivery boys coming to the house, Kreck had to shop each day, a task that made him so irritable that I offered to help him. Herr Metzenburg, who saw us one afternoon as we returned to the house with our parcels, thanked me for helping, but told me that he did not wish me to walk alone in the city, although a stroll in the nearby Tiergarten would be safe. There had been acts of violence that summer against Jewish shopkeepers, and I noticed that many windows and doors in the shopping district were marked with crude drawings and inscriptions.

Kreck, despite Herr Metzenburg's warning, began to send me on errands alone, and I soon learned my way along the streets and alleys. Although I was frightened at first, especially on the streets that had been looted, and worried that I would be lost or stopped by the gangs of men I saw in the street, I felt useful and efficient, checking off the errands on my list as I proudly instructed the shopkeepers to charge my purchases to the Metzenburgs' account.

I wrote to Mr. Knox describing the Tickell's thrush, red-headed buntings, and icterine warbler I saw in the Tiergarten. I also told him about the ruined shops and frightening caricatures on the walls of the buildings. When I read the letter for spelling errors, I was surprised by its worried tone. I didn't want Mr. Knox to think that I was afraid, or in danger, and I copied the letter onto a new sheet of paper, leaving out the description of the shops.

. . .

As we wrapped the last of the Vincennes, Kreck said, "I'm surprised that Herr Metzenburg hasn't received another visit from Herr Hofer. He came once, but did not remain more than a few minutes." He made a face, but I couldn't tell if he was disappointed or relieved. "It's well known that our Führer doesn't admire the Romanesque, in which Herr Metzenburg has a particular interest, although Reichsmarschall Göring has a passion for it. He has coveted Herr Felix's collection since the old days. It is thanks in part to the Reichsmarschall that prices are so high." He also said, lowering his voice, that one of the Reichsmarschall's friends in the Foreign Office had that week offered Herr Metzenburg a posting in Algiers. Although Herr Felix refused to leave Germany, he did not wish to prevent Frau Metzenburg from going, if that was what she desired. Kreck said that Herr Felix wanted to be with his treasures, but Frau Metzenburg wanted to be with Herr Felix. Sometimes, Kreck said, Herr Felix acted as if his objects had lives of their own. I was curious to know more, but two porters came into the room to remove a crate, and Kreck fell silent.

We moved to Löwendorf at the end of October, traveling in two cars, one of them driven by Herr Felix. A few boys were standing at the gates when we arrived, shoulders hunched with the chill, and a white-haired man from the village, Herr Pflüger, waited hat in hand in the gravel court in front of the house. He insisted on helping with the numerous suitcases, and I could see that Kreck didn't like it.

The house, known as the Yellow Palace, was a large, square, symmetrical box of yellow stone in the classical style, two stories high, with marble urns at the corners of the flat roof. On the ground floor, five arched windows, their shutters painted sea green, looked onto a terrace with marble statues. There was a park with a narrow river running through it, and at the bottom of the park, a small temple with a striped awning on its roof. A large house, the Pavilion, built for Frau Metzenburg's parents when they married, was in the park and, in the distance, a forest called the Night Wood.

Kreck, who'd been sent to Löwendorf ahead of us to see to the unloading of twenty-three wagons of treasure, took me through the rooms. The house had been built by a student of Karl Friedrich Schinkel for Frau Metzenburg's great-grandmother, the Baroness Schumacher. There was gold-and-black lacquer furniture in the dining room and music room, and a chandelier with fifty-six candles in the hall. The walls of the dining room were painted with Chinese figures, outlined in silver. A low divan of white silk ran along two sides of the drawing room, whose walls were covered with rectangles of pale green silk framed in gold. In the paneled library, there were lime-wood bookcases, two desks, leather chairs, and a long table for reading maps and manuscripts. In each of the rooms, Kreck had filled pale green vases with leafless stalks of allium, the only flower that Herr Felix allowed in the house in winter.

My bedroom was on the second floor, overlooking the avenue of Dutch elms. The curtains and bed coverings were in pale blue linen. There was a black marble fireplace and a red-and-orange patterned carpet. Against one wall was a chest of drawers. A gilt mirror above the chimneypiece reflected the tops of the elms. I could see the river, winding through the park, and the two German oaks that stood on either side of a brick path leading to a large cobblestoned stable yard with a clock tower. Beyond the stables were a walled kitchen garden and a garage. An allée of box led to a plantation of mulberry trees. There was a large orchard of cherry, apple, pear, and plum trees and, beyond it, a fenced meadow, used as a paddock for the horses.

Although the beautiful rooms were a bit dusty, the garden a bit wild (Kreck told me that nothing had been changed at Löwendorf in a hundred years), the Yellow Palace was the most *vorzügliche* place I'd ever seen.

Seven of us lived at Löwendorf—the Metzenburgs, Fräulein Roeder, Kreck, Schmidt the cook, myself, and a young man from the village named Caspar Boerner, who was the gamekeeper. Herr Felix's donkey, Zara, and seven dogs were kept in the stables with the horses.

It was hoped that Caspar Boerner would be able to assume some of the simpler tasks of Herr Felix's valet, as well as those of the footman, both of whom had been mobilized along with the farmworkers, gardeners, and grooms. Caspar, who was nineteen years old, lived with his widowed mother in a farmhouse near the village. His two brothers had been conscripted, but Caspar was exempt from military service, at least for the moment, thanks to the loss of three fingers on his right hand.

Kreck said that it was bad enough without servants, but with only Caspar to help in the Yellow Palace, it would be a *Katastrophe*. Caspar, whose cropped hair was the color and texture of swans' down, had lost his fingers in an otter trap. As the Reich was opposed to cruelty in all forms, Herr Felix thought it best that no one know the details of his accident, as just that month a man in Potsdam had been sentenced to four months in prison for throwing stones at a bird (Roeder hinted that Caspar had injured himself on purpose—Caspar's brother, according to her, was a Communist).

Kreck said that no one in Caspar's family had ever been a house servant, the Boerners fit only for fieldwork, and he wondered if Caspar's new responsibilities would be too difficult for him, the boy more adept at twisting the neck of a pheasant than winding a cravat around Herr Felix's neck. Herr Felix had a very precise morning routine, including the playing of jazz records as he dressed, but Kreck suspected that Caspar had never even seen a gramophone (Kreck, himself very fond of a band called the Weintraub Syncopators, had brought several boxes of gramophone needles with him from Berlin). Caspar, who moved into a room over the stables, would also serve as groom, cut and store wood, and polish our boots when we left them outside our doors at night. He would take me to the village in the dogcart when I needed to buy anything of a personal nature. In the village, which was three miles away, there was a church, a blacksmith, a mill, a baker, a dry-goods store, and a small inn.

·　　·　　·

I didn't like to think of myself as a servant, but I knew that I fell into that less easily defined company that included governesses and ladies' maids. It was Catholic girls who went out as servants, not Palmers (a thought that sounded so alarmingly like my mother that I immediately put it out of my head). It was to the Metzenburgs' credit that they did not live by the more simple rules that governed domestic life in Ireland. Because her wealth served to isolate her, Frau Metzenburg did not trouble with the customary prejudices of her class. Herr Felix, despite the railroads in South America, and a boyhood position akin to godhead in a house of doting women, was unusual in that neither money nor adoration had ruined him. Although the distinctions between master and servant were maintained in traditional ways—the taking of meals, forms of address (I called them Dorothea and Felix only in my head), clothing—as well as a more subtle sublimation of self, I was surprised by their courtesy (the best manners in Europe). But I counted myself so fortunate to have escaped Ballycarra that I would have endured anything.

At night when the house was quiet, I would arrange the silver dish and the gold pen and the cigarette holder, as well as a pair of doeskin gloves I'd found drying in the laundry, around my room. (As I didn't intend to keep the lovely objects, I didn't consider myself a thief.) My rash decision to accompany Countess Inéz to Berlin had been made in ignorance, I knew, but I did not regret it. The disturbing restlessness of my girlhood was gone, my longing replaced by the sense that a world in which anything might happen had opened to me and, even more astonishing, that I'd been allowed to enter it. It cannot be chance that my favorite book that winter was *All This, and Heaven Too*, in which a French nobleman murders his wife in order to marry the governess.

As I didn't speak German, Herr Felix arranged for me to spend an hour each afternoon with Herr Elias, whom Felix had recently brought from Berlin when the Ministry of Information drafted his secretary. I found Caspar lurking in the library when I arrived for my first lesson, dusting books as he sang a ditty in German. He grinned when he saw me and sang the verse again. When Herr Elias came into the library a few minutes later, Caspar abruptly stopped singing, although apparently not soon enough. Herr Elias said something to him, and Caspar lowered his head and went back to work.

Kreck had told me that Herr Elias's father was Italian, which explained his dark eyes and thick black hair, but he put me more in mind of the Saracen warrior Saladin, whose adventures I'd followed in Mr. Knox's book about the Crusades. Although Herr Elias did not have the easy elegance of Herr Felix, there was a manliness about him that I found most engaging.

Kreck also said that Herr Elias was fortunate to be alive. In early November, a Jew had been accused of murdering a German diplomat in Paris, and Nazi storm troopers, assisted by enraged citizens, had looted and set fire to many Jewish shops and houses in Berlin. A synagogue on Fasanenstrasse had been burned to the ground, and another in Savignyplatz.

Women had roamed the streets with empty prams, the better to load them with looted goods. Thousands of Jews had been arrested and sent to Sachsenhausen prison in the north of the city. "You're not a Jehovah's Witness, are you?" Kreck asked, peering at me. He made me think that I could end up in Sachsenhausen—that we all could end up in Sachsenhausen.

Dorothea's grandmother had liked to mark the year with saints' feast days and festivals, and on Christmas Eve, the villagers had visited the Yellow Palace to drink *Weihnachtspunsch* and to sing carols. As Dorothea wished to continue the tradition, a big spruce was cut in the Night Wood on the second Sunday of Advent. Roeder and I decorated the tree with the baroness's collection of Neapolitan ornaments, and Kreck prepared baskets of ham and schnapps for the families of the workers on the estate. As I hung branches of holly in the dining room, I had a sudden longing for home. Although I didn't miss the gray winters of Ballycarra or the cold pews in Mr. Knox's stone church or the awkward exchange of practical presents Christmas morning (with the special treat of a glass of sherry and an orange), I felt sad at the thought of my mother and father.

It was very cold that first winter at Löwendorf. It snowed for weeks, softening all sound but for the constant roar of the wind from the east. The river was frozen, and in the park, the trees splintered and cracked in two. Caspar and I trudged through the fresh snow with long poles to knock the snow from the branches of the fruit trees. As we swung our poles, the snow flying through the cold air, the crows lifted themselves noisily into the sky. The boys from the village sometimes followed us, unable to resist pelting us with snow, and we chased them across the frozen meadow, shouting with happiness.

1939

In the new year, Dorothea engaged some women and old men from the village to work as laundresses, kitchen maids, and gardeners. I was put to work in the library, helping Herr Elias to separate those books collected by Dorothea's mother from Herr Elias's own rare and valuable books. There was a gramophone in the library as well as in the drawing room and in Felix's dressing room, and Herr Elias played music as we worked, beginning the day with *Dido and Aeneas* and ending with Django Reinhardt.

Although I was sometimes asked to mend a torn curtain hem or one of Felix's jackets (Caspar too busy dusting books), the making of lace was never mentioned. I'd once thought of nothing but lace (and of escape, the two linked in my mind). I'd seen patterns everywhere—in Mr. Knox's handwriting, in nests, in the wings of a mayfly and the scales of a trout—and I felt uneasy without a piece of lace in my hands. I often dreamed that I had unraveled a piece of lace in the park, the white silk strung through the trees like a web. My hands, no longer sore and swollen, seemed to belong to a stranger.

Aside from the works of Karl May, many of Frau Schumacher's books were about horses or missionaries, and many of them were in English. I sometimes took books to my room— *Oil for the Lamps of China*, *The Painted Veil*, and *The Bridge of Desire*—books that were a revelation after George Eliot and Mrs. Gaskell. In an attempt to be friendly, I asked Roeder (she was on her way from church in the village and seemed slightly less disdainful than usual) if she'd like to read a book from the library, but she said that she found the Book of Life entirely sufficient for her needs. I disliked her intensely (I worried at first that she'd notice, until I realized that she didn't care in the least). Kreck told me that she had inherited her position as lady's maid from her own mother, who had served Dorothea's mother for sixty years until her death. Her many fears were as real to her as the *Almanach de Gotha*. When she came upon a thorn bush in which the carcasses of small birds and frogs were impaled, she announced that a spell had been cast on the Yellow Palace, hinting that the foreign princess, as she called Inéz, had been practicing black magic again. She refused to believe me when I explained that the little corpses were merely the leftovers of the greedy shrike, kept for another day's feast, and she took to wearing two gold crosses around her neck.

.   .   .

When Herr Elias asked me to tell him a story in German, Caspar, who somehow contrived to be in the library each afternoon during my lesson, noticed my reluctance and quickly offered to tell a story in my place. Herr Elias said that he would like to hear Caspar's story, but he still expected me to take my turn. A grinning Caspar stood before us, hands clasped at his waist, and began to speak.

"I've been hunting in the Night Wood all my life, first using a slingshot made by my late beloved father and later a rifle given to him by Frau Schumacher in gratitude for saving one of her dogs from drowning. We weren't starving—my father died from wounds suffered in the Great War when I was ten years old—but my mother relied on the rabbits and birds I brought home to feed us. Most of the game at Löwendorf had been killed off before I was born, and the one remaining gamekeeper spent his days sleeping in a forester's hut. I went into the woods whenever I liked. When the coachman, who had quarreled with my father over politics, caught me one night with a bag of squirrels, I was sure I'd be beaten, but after only a few blows, he took me by the ear to Frau Schumacher, who then and there made me her new gamekeeper. It seems she had a madness for roast squirrel."

"It's the beginning of a fairy tale," I said in German, with the help of a dictionary. To my relief, our time had come to an end. I could conjugate verbs and even recite some poetry, but I didn't like to talk about myself—it was only thanks to Mr. Knox that I had conversation in English. As I hastily gathered my books, Herr Elias said to me, "Don't think that you'll escape every time, Fräulein," and he and Caspar had a good laugh, irritating me, as I couldn't imagine that Caspar had understood him.

The next day, Herr Elias lit a cigarette, and the two men (Caspar arriving just in time) settled themselves at the library table. Kreck brought a pot of black-currant tea and seed cake each afternoon, and Herr Elias poured himself a cup of tea.

I hadn't slept, writing and then learning my speech by heart, and I was a bit shaky. I pushed back my chair and began. "I was taught to fish by Mr. Hugh Knox when I was a child, using my grandfather's salmon flies, and his bamboo rod, which was nine feet long and too heavy for me. Mr. Knox would cast into the Ridge Pool and I would guide the line between my fingers as he slowly turned the reel. Later, he made a rod for me that was more suitable to my size and I began to catch small muddy trout of my own." I paused for breath. Some of the vocabulary was difficult—*Lachsfliegen, kleine schlammige Forellen, geeignet*— and I was uncertain of my grammar, my Irish accent rendering some of the words incomprehensible, but both my tormentors looked pleased, even interested, and I continued. "My father and mother had no interest in the river. We lived in rooms above my father's shop. My grandmother died of consumption when my mother was a girl, and she lived in fear of catching the disease. I wasn't allowed to play with the Catholic children, and my only companion was Mr. Knox. My mother was relieved to have me taken off her hands, and I was grateful to be gone. When I returned from my walks with Mr. Knox, she would ask if I'd been near the village children, and I would say that I had not, even when I'd passed them in the road. I often imagined what it would be like if the germs killed my mother. I would live with Mr. Knox and I would be happy."

Caspar and Herr Elias were no longer lounging in their chairs but sat with straight backs, staring at me with solemn faces. Herr Elias's tea was untouched. Neither of them spoke for a moment. Then Herr Elias said, "Thank you, Fräulein. *Sie überraschen mich immer wieder.* You surprise me again and again."

All that Caspar said was *"Ich wusste nicht, dass Sie angeln Können."* I didn't know you could fish.

My reading that summer, thanks to Herr Elias, who loaned me novels (I'd quickly grown bored with Frau Schumacher's books), had grown to include stories that Mr. Knox would have considered very exotic. Other than the fairy tales, there'd been nothing but English and Irish books in Mr. Knox's library, with few German characters.

I noticed that many of the young men in Herr Elias's books begin their careers with love affairs with older women— Rousseau's *Confessions, The Red and the Black, The Charterhouse of Parma* (his aunt!), and *Lost Illusions,* among others. When I asked Herr Elias about this, he said that it was what they did in France. When I reminded him that *The Charterhouse of Parma* is set in Italy, he said, "There, too."

At his suggestion, I read *Effie Briest* (slowly and with his help), in hope of better acquainting myself with German literature. The book made me long for a lover of my own and, even more, I longed for the wiles I imagined necessary to hold such a lover. The story made me wish that I were beautiful. Herr Elias was often in my dreams (I no longer dreamed about lace), so you might say that we spent quite a bit of time together.

Like Felix, Herr Elias had a passion for music, and I began to make a tray cloth for him with a *punto in aria* pattern of musical instruments—it was the first lace I'd sewn in some time— but I had to put it aside when Dorothea asked me to make a pair of trousers for her. I knew little about sewing clothes, but I began by taking her measurements. I was unaccustomed to seeing women in their underwear (she stood calmly in her peach silk knickers). It wasn't her lack of modesty that made me uncomfortable but her evident disdain. She seemed to be defying me to blush, and I'm pleased to say that while it was a struggle, I did not oblige her.

On the first day of September, a distraught Kreck rushed into the sewing room to tell me that Germany had invaded Poland. He said that Herr Felix was waiting to speak to us in the library. I rose immediately, my apron dotted with blood— I'd pricked myself when he told me the news—and followed him downstairs.

Herr Felix was at his desk. Dorothea was not there. Schmidt, Caspar, and Roeder stood together, and Kreck and I took our places beside them. Felix said that we were free, of course, to return to our homes now that Germany was at war. He understood that I might be particularly alarmed to find myself at Löwendorf at such a perilous moment. He was relieved that he and Frau Metzenburg had left Berlin, especially as some of their friends had begun to disappear simply because their names were in the wrong address books. Although his voice was calm, I noticed that his hands were shaking when he picked up a newspaper he'd been reading. There appears to be a new law, he said. "Forbidding Jews to own—" He stopped to read directly from the paper. "Radios and—"

Roeder interrupted him to say that her place was with Frau Metzenburg. Schmidt and Caspar also said that they did not wish to leave Löwendorf. Kreck, whose face was wet with tears, said nothing, and Felix turned to me.

Caspar, his blue eyes narrowed with expectation, nodded at me in encouragement, but Roeder had difficulty concealing the smirk of superiority that implied that she'd taken me for a bolter from the start. Schmidt seemed distracted, gazing in wonder at the row of Meissen pagodas. When I said that I, too, chose to remain at Löwendorf, Caspar dropped his head in relief. Felix, impassively prepared for a different answer, thanked me. He said that he would do all that he could to keep us safe. As we left the library, Kreck took me aside to say that Herr Metzenburg had many friends in the diplomatic corps and in the Ministry of Foreign Affairs and that because of this, he knew things that the rest of us could not possibly know. He said that I should do whatever Herr Felix asked me to do, no matter how implausible.

Later, when I took up my sewing, my hands, too, were shaking, and I was unable to thread my needle. I understood nothing of Germany and the forces that had brought her to war. For the first time, I regretted the hours I'd spent reading French novels, rather than the newspaper. Although I sometimes read the paper from Hamburg (it was one of the German exercises given me by Herr Elias), I'd been more interested in the views of my companions than in news of the world. That Felix had declined the offer of an important post abroad seemed to indicate his opinion of the Reich. I knew that Kreck had been with Herr Felix since Felix was at university, and that he'd lost his eye in 1916 in service to the emperor (he'd said more than once that he had no intention of losing his other eye for his own or any other country). Fräulein Roeder, who'd tended Dorothea since she was sent as a girl to live with her grandfather in London, did not hesitate to express her admiration of Hitler's frequent speeches, particularly the one in which the Führer said that the geniality, diligence, and steadfastness of the German people would be harnessed for works of peace and human culture, but Roeder did not exhibit any signs of the Führer lovesickness that I'd noticed in other German ladies (when she said that many Nazis were, in fact, practicing Christians, Felix closed his eyes, his hand on his forehead, and nodded). Her favorite nephew had been mobilized that winter, and she frequently sent him packages—I saw her in the village when I was posting my letters to Mr. Knox.

I doubted if Caspar supported the Nazis. He was infuriated by the stories he heard of Nazi brutality. His older brother was in the Wehrmacht. His younger brother had been arrested for distributing political pamphlets and taken to Plötzensee prison, and there had been no word of him for weeks. I was from a country that declared itself neutral, and my opinions were naturally of little interest to anyone. As for Dorothea, I had no idea what she thought.

My mother liked to claim that a gossip was merely someone who took a healthy and even gainful interest in life, which, of course, allowed her to say whatever she liked, but the gossip in my village was not like the gossip at Löwendorf. If a person managed to escape from Ballycarra, he fled to Philadelphia or London or Sydney, rarely to be seen again—it mattered little to him what people said about him. Few strangers stopped in Ballycarra—perhaps every generation, a wife or two was brought from a nearby town, but no more than that. Gossip tended to have some truth in it, as nothing could remain hidden for long. Mrs. Cumming's husband beat her. The doctor was drinking himself to death. At Löwendorf, the opposite was true. Rumors were naturally concerned with matters far more grave than the increasing frequency of Dr. Fiske's visits to the pub, and nothing could be known for certain.

Although Germany was at war, our life at Löwendorf continued in the same slow fashion. There were moments, however, when I was reminded that we were not as safe as we appeared to be. During a lesson, Herr Elias said that I might want to exercise a certain skepticism in regard to the German words that I was learning—I could begin with *Vaterland*. When I asked what he meant, he said, "Surely, *meine liebe*, you know that I am a Jew." I blushed and said that I had not known that he was a Jew. He said nothing more, and I continued my translation of "Puss 'n Boots."

It seemed to me that many people, including myself, didn't know the first thing about Jews—what they believed or how

they thought. I often heard women in the village frightening their children with the threat that the Jews would get
them if they didn't do as they were told. When I asked Caspar
about this, he shrugged and said that German mothers had
always been that way. When I pressed him further, he said
that while he himself wouldn't use such threats, he couldn't
vouch for the trustworthiness of all Jews. When I asked if he
could vouch for the trustworthiness of all Germans, he didn't
answer me.

I understood that I lived in a house of spies (I heard Kreck
say that it was nothing to him, as we lived in a country of spies),
but I also knew that we did not spy for gain or even for our
beliefs. We spied because it eased our fear—even though any
secrets we might chance to discover were of a domestic nature,
and of no possible interest to anyone but ourselves (and often
not even then). Roeder told me that Herr Felix had refused
to engage any new servants long before the start of the war,
after he twice caught footmen listening at doors. They must
have looked like kingfishers in their livery of blue tailcoats and
gold waistcoats, bent at the waist, heads cocked as they peered
through keyholes.

Schmidt watched Kreck. Kreck watched Caspar. Caspar
watched me. Roeder watched Dorothea. Dorothea watched
Felix. I watched all of them (I was sent one day to Felix's
dressing room when he forgot his riding gloves, and I held
his enamel cufflinks, one of them depicting the night sky and
its constellations, the other a miniature globe of the world,
and slipped one of his batiste handkerchiefs into my pocket
before grabbing the gloves and quickly closing the drawer, but

I wouldn't have called that spying). If Herr Felix watched any-one, he was good at concealing it.

When Roeder knocked on the door of the sewing room—I'd finished Dorothea's trousers and was mending a cushion—I thought at first that she'd come to collect the cap she'd asked me to make for her niece's baby, rather insultingly offering to pay me in buttons, an arrangement I had declined. She had then offered me cash money, an offer that she also expected me to decline, which I did. She knew that I would make the cap, given the intimacy of the household and our growing dependence on one another. The cap was easy enough to sew, taking me only a few evenings' work, but I resented every stitch.

She was on her way to evensong at St. Adalbert's (I could hear the bells). Her undersized black hat, two lace lappets hanging on either side of her whiskered face, turned her into an elderly black hare. She stood in the center of the room, her gloved hands folded across her little bulging belly, and said that she wished to be certain that I understood that Frau Metzenburg's great-grandmother had not been a Jew, despite the lies spread by the wicked. The Schumachers, who were bankers, had been given a Certificate of True Belief when they converted to the Christian faith at the beginning of the nineteenth century. Frau Metzenburg's great-grandfather, the old baron, had been financial adviser to Queen Victoria, and her grandmother was by birth a baroness. "There are rumors to this day," said Roeder, working a loose hatpin into her head, "that

Prince Albert himself was the unhappy result of a friendship between his mother and her Jewish chamberlain. A story that I have always refused to believe." She made the small curtsy she executed whenever she mentioned the royal family of any country, lifting her black dress a few inches from the floor.

I gave her the little cap and she thanked me. She said that Frau Metzenburg was driving to Potsdam in the morning and would like me to accompany her. I was surprised, as Roeder often chose not to tell me when Dorothea asked for me, and I realized that she must had been scolded for her forgetfulness, which would not have improved her disposition.

Inéz stopped at Löwendorf that first Christmas of the war on her way to Munich, where she was hoping to collect her two children to take them to safety in Cairo. I was surprised to learn that she had children, as she had never mentioned them. Count Hartenfels was refusing to let the children leave Germany, and Inéz was dining with Reichsmarschall Göring to ask him to use his influence with her former husband. Felix thought there was a good chance that Göring would help her, as he'd once said that he found it unsportsmanlike to kill children.

As Inéz was superstitious, I was summoned at the last minute to join the Metzenburgs and their guests at Christmas lunch—there were to be fourteen, but a friend driving from Berlin had been delayed ("More like arrested," Kreck whispered to me). I patted Hungarian water on my less-than-clean hair and put on my best skirt—not good enough, I knew, but I also knew that no one would look at me twice—and hurried to the winter dining room.

An expressionless Kreck, his hands shaking in his white cotton gloves, moved haltingly around the table as he slid plates past the gesticulating guests. Caspar, dressed by Kreck in the footman's livery, filled glasses with champagne. We were having smoked trout, partridges, potatoes Anna, and brussels sprouts, with apple tart for dessert, everything grown or killed on the estate. In the center of the table, four porcelain pheasants and a large porcelain turkey cock sat in nests of holly. On a sideboard, a rhinoceros, a monkey, a ram, a fawn, and a lion, all in glazed bisque, stood around the tiny silver-and-velvet bed I'd packed in Berlin, patiently waiting for the Christ Child to arrive. On the walls, bunches of mistletoe and rowanberries were joined by swags of oak leaves. At the top of each plate was a small lapis bowl holding a pale green hellebore set in ice that had been shaved to resemble snow. Candles had been lit, as it would be dark by the middle of the afternoon.

I was seated next to Felix's old tutor from Heidelberg, Herr Professor Sigmund Wasselmann, who shook with cold despite the heat from the enamel stove in the corner. He was so thin that his green jacket with horn buttons looked several sizes too large for him (unlike Caspar, whose chamois breeches were a size too small). Professor Wasselmann, who had stayed at Löwendorf that summer, glanced sternly around the room, his large hands folding and refolding a sheet of blue writing paper. He waited until all of the women were safely in their chairs, then sat down, tucking his large napkin into his collar. The

woman on his right, whose name was Mary Barnard according
to her place card, and who was dressed in a man's tweed suit
and striped tie, spoke to the professor in Latin.

Don Jaime, a son of the king of Spain, was on my left (Roeder
had hurriedly whispered to me that Don Jaime would one day,
as Henri VI, be heir to the throne of France, even though he
could neither speak nor hear). Across from me was a handsome young man in the uniform of an army staff officer. I saw
instantly that he was glamorous. His elegance of form and his
nonchalant yet haughty assumption of masculine power were
pleasantly disturbing, and I steeled myself to resist him.

Inéz, who was next to the young officer, had spent the night
in Berlin. She looked particularly beautiful in a cream wool
suit weighted with two large emerald clips. She gleamed across
the table at me and said, "My dear, the city is *overrun* with
fortune-tellers. It always happens. I've seen it before." Despite
all that Inéz had done for me and, I was sure, for others, I'd
begun to feel a bit weary of her. She spoke and moved as if she
meant to be admired (she was rarely disappointed), and I'd
found myself refusing to attend to her during her brief visits
(more like incarnations). I'd begun to wonder if I were envious
of her—like most people with charm, she required an atmo-
sphere of adoration to stimulate and satisfy her, and it could be
tiring. Before I could answer her, she turned to the officer, her
hand resting lightly on his wrist.

On Don Jaime's other side was Maria Milde, who had
arrived with the officer. I'd seen Maria Milde's movie *Winter
Carousel* in Berlin the year before, and although the story, a
musical comedy, was sentimental, I admired Maria Milde very

much. I knew that she lived at the Jagdschloss Glienicke near the bridge in Babelsberg because I'd read it in a film magazine (she was being groomed at Ufa Studios as the Reich's answer to Greta Garbo), which, though censored, was still published for the good of our morale. There was something winning about her, in addition to her beauty—her pinched nostrils gave her a slight look of disgust—and I had to keep myself from staring (Caspar, who hovered behind us, not only did not look at Fräulein Milde, he did not, to my annoyance, look at me— I wasn't seeking his admiration but his complicity). Her thin lips were the color of lavender—I'd learned from Inéz that lavender lips (she considered it her husband's only physical flaw) were the sign of an opium addict. As I studied her hair, which was pulled into a silver snood at the nape of her neck, I heard her tell Don Jaime that she lived with ten other young actresses in the castle in Babelsberg. "I've decided to be a most unreasonable roommate," she said with a sly smile, "so that when I am famous, they will already dislike me." Undeterred by his silence, she said that her ermine stole had been a Christmas gift from the officer, turning to blow him a little kiss across the table, which he ignored. Don Jaime, increasingly agitated, seemed to be reaching a state of near exaltation, which confused me, given his condition.

On the other side of Fräulein Milde was Felix's lawyer, Hans Koch, with whom Felix had been at school as a boy. I knew Herr Koch, as he came to the Yellow Palace every few weeks, when he and Felix would lock themselves in the library for the day. Herr Koch had difficulty getting Maria Milde's attention, taken as she was with Don Jaime, and he soon turned to the dark-haired woman on his other side, a journalist named Hilde Meisel. Fraülein Meisel was wearing the chicest hat I'd ever seen—I could tell that even Inéz envied it from her expression when they were introduced. The hat of black tulle, raven feathers, and velvet pompoms did not accentuate her plainness, as sometimes happens, but turned her into a creature of enchantment.

At the end of the table were a husband and wife, Herr and Frau Prazan, cousins of Felix, who had arrived unexpectedly, and sat on either side of him. They were traveling from Hamburg to their estate near Prague and carried letters to Felix from his sister, who had left the country for Argentina. Their arrival made my presence no longer necessary, but no one seemed to notice.

I recognized Count von Arnstadt, who'd come frequently to Löwendorf that autumn. He worked for the Ministry of Information as editor of the Reich's magazine *Berlin-Rome-Tokio*. Herr Elias had translated one of the count's controversial articles for me, entitled "The Third World War," in which he claimed that should the United States ever enter the war, it would emerge the most powerful nation in the world. He believed that the fury with which Russia and America were bound to clash would be far more threatening to peace than any conceivable conflict among England, the Continent, and Russia.

"Every few days," I heard Arnstadt say to Dorothea, his face twitching with mischief, "I find myself in the cramped office of the Head of Section, where I am left to study in solitude the Little Friend, which is my name for the log of telephone conversations gathered each week by the Gestapo. Most of it I cannot repeat, as it consists of the highly indiscreet conversations of most of our friends and their lovers. Each Friday, after a most careful reading, I prepare a copy of the transcripts for the Führer—double spaced and in bold type—which is rushed by hand to the Chancellery. He can hardly wait to receive it." The count seemed careful not to appear in earnest, causing me to wonder if that was why he was considered the most amusing man in Berlin. I thought that his mild mockery of the Gestapo and even the Führer was a sign that he trusted the Metzenburgs and their guests. I also wondered if it were a trap. It was exciting to think that anyone at the table (although perhaps not the professor) might be a spy.

Across from me, Inéz described the dinner that had been given in her honor the night before. Her friend Danielle Darrieux had been there, and they'd danced to Cuban music on the gramophone. Their host, the tireless Japanese ambassador Mr. Oshima, had arranged a shooting match with air guns, and Inéz had won second prize, which was a bottle of Chanel No. 5—Serge Lifar, another guest, had cheated, according to a still-angry Inéz, winning first prize of a bottle of perfume, a powder puff, *and* a pair of stockings. Later they'd gone to a nightclub in Kurfürstendamm. "A towering Negro woman, the last black left in Berlin, danced with a white horse," said Inéz.

"I don't think she means 'danced,' " Herr Koch said mysteriously to Hilde Meisel.

As Inéz described the horse (she found the Negro woman a bit coarse), I felt something brush against my leg. I thought, given the circumstances, that someone might be trying to signal me, and I sneaked a glance under the tablecloth. A slender foot—the toenails painted crimson and encased in a pale silk stocking—darted from between Don Jaime's shaking knees and disappeared.

Don Jaime, who had been following Inéz's every gesture with a concentration so intense that I feared he might explode, tried with no success to catch her eye. As she was careful to beguile everyone in sight, I wondered if Spain had offended her by behaving badly to Cuba, then quickly dismissed the idea. Inéz did not take sides. Suddenly, Don Jaime thrust a hand in her direction, interrupting her and compelling her at last to look at him. She waited—we all waited—but Don Jaime was silent.

I'd noticed Professor Wasselmann eyeing Maria Milde's plate of uneaten food for some time (he was a little drunk), and without thinking, perhaps because Don Jaime was making me nervous, I reached across him to exchange Fräulein Milde's plate for the professor's empty plate. To my relief, Fräulein Milde behaved as if it had been her idea, beaming with condescension as the professor whisked the last of her potatoes into his mouth.

The officer (Maria Milde, perhaps in explanation of his rudeness, had announced that he was a Battenberg prince) lit a cigarette with a silver field lighter. Smoke streaming from his mouth, he leaned across the table. "Our Führer," he said in English, "does not take kindly to princes of the blood like myself in the field, and he would deny us our ancient and honored privilege of dying in battle. Sons of noble families are forbidden to serve at the front, but I have thought of nothing but war since I was a boy. I have been trained for nothing else. Dreamed of nothing else. The Führer has robbed my life of all meaning, while he talks aloud to the portrait of Frederick the Great he keeps at his side." He pushed back his chair and strode from the table, Maria Milde following him anxiously with her eyes, as Caspar hurried to open the door for him. Don Jaime jumped to his feet and rushed around the table to take the officer's empty chair, and Inéz, at last, turned to him with a smile, causing Don Jaime to fall back in his chair.

I knew that Felix did not like political talk at the table, but there was little he could do to prevent it. He looked ill at ease, which wasn't like him. He was inclined to indulge the comfort of others, if only to alleviate his boredom. His politeness, I'd come to realize, served, among other things, to afford him the distance that he preferred and even required. As Kreck carried an apple tart to the table, a young, pleasant-looking couple who I assumed were newlyweds, so intent were they on each other, arrived with shy apologies and sat in two chairs alongside Dorothea. Kreck told me later that they were the children of Felix's boyhood music teacher, who'd been arrested in Regensburg in November. Felix had arranged for them to travel to Algiers with the exit visas that his friend in the Foreign Office had obtained for him and Dorothea, should they ever need them.

Maria Milde leaned toward Don Jaime. "In my experience," she said as if imparting a secret, "it is the Dutch and the Norwegians who hate us the most. The French, as I'm sure you know, like us the very best."

To my relief, I heard Felix's familiar cultivated voice. "In 1918, when I was twenty years old, I was so ashamed of our country that my father's death at the Somme was in some ways a relief. If he had survived, I would have held him, along with my uncles and the rest of his generation, responsible for the horror of the war. In those days, we schoolboys no longer trusted our elders who, in any talk of the reasons for our country's shame, always avoided the truth by claiming that there was nothing they could have done to stop it." He paused. "When I was older, I realized that schoolboys in England and France and Turkey must have felt just as I did. Some now say that our friends in France yearn for a quick German victory simply because they cannot bear the responsibility of another million killed in battle. We are in the same position as those men we once blamed, only it is we who are at fault, we who are making the same mistakes as our fathers so that our country can bring about another fatal catastrophe. And what is one to do? To leave Germany is inconceivable. All we can know for certain is that the abyss awaits us."

Even Kreck had stopped moving. No one spoke for a moment, and then I heard Maria Milde ask Don Jaime, "Am I dreaming, or was that potato pie we had for lunch?"

As I looked around the table, I reminded myself that on a dark winter's day in Ballycarra, just such an afternoon, with film stars, champagne, and handsome princes, had been all that I desired.

After the guests at last left (they stayed for hours, Caspar making several trips to the Pavilion for more wine), I helped Kreck and Caspar to clear the table. I needed Caspar's help to carry the turkey cock to the pantry where it was put away (Felix told Kreck that it would be the last lunch party at Löwendorf for some time), but I was able to do the rest myself. Under Professor Wasselmann's immaculate plate, I found a small, folded sheet of blue writing paper. I opened it and read it. I could understand certain words—the words "tank," "batallion," and "munition" are the same in English—and I quickly put the note in my pocket. That there really had been a spy at Christmas lunch was exciting. That it was Professor Wasselmann was a shock.

Later that evening, I passed Felix on my way to the sewing room, having vowed at lunch to make a lace dinner dress for myself. When I stopped to thank him, he said, "You *see* what we do? We celebrate the low, and we long for the past. I'd hoped to be done with deception. My own as well as others." He was very upset.

"Deception?" I asked.

"That everything will be well for us. That the old world will survive. That it deserves to survive."

Before I could answer, not that I had an answer, he bid me good night and disappeared down the passage.

The next morning, Kreck brought me a long bundle wrapped in bleached muslin. There was a note tucked into the muslin. It was from Inéz, who had written under an engraved coronet, *My dear, as I will be taking my children with me when I leave Munich, I have no room for these—might you not wear them for me?* Inside the bundle were two blouses, one of natural raw silk with capped sleeves, the other with tiny pleats of Moroccan crepe, long sleeves, and round pearl buttons. There was a pair of lilac suede gloves, a black suit with a hint of a peplum, a gray pongee suit with a chinchilla collar, a black wool afternoon dress with a wide belt and white faille collar and cuffs, two pairs of stockings (pale, sheer), and a pair of black alligator pumps with rounded toes. Labels were sewn into the seams of the clothes—SCHIAPARELLI, DOUCET, LANVIN—with Inéz's initials and the date that they had been made for her (I was the same size as Inéz, although smaller in the bust). I fell back on the bed, my new clothes clasped in my arms.

As I slipped on the shoes—they were too big, and I would have to stuff the toes with cotton—I promised never again to criticize her. As I tried on the black suit in the mirror, I swore that I would never again think ill of her or, for that matter, anyone. It was the first time in my life that I'd been given anything so beautiful. I didn't for an instant believe that she hadn't room in her luggage.

1940

The smiling brother and sister who were at Christmas lunch left for Spain at the end of March, hoping to make their way to Algiers. Dorothea was angry when she discovered that Felix had given them the passes, perhaps imagining that they themselves might one day use them. It was the only quarrel I ever knew them to have—whether to fly to safety or to stay at Löwendorf. Once Felix gave away the passes, it would be difficult for the Metzenburgs to leave the country. Kreck told me that Dorothea had considered for a moment going to Copenhagen, where she had cousins, but the Nazis invaded Denmark the first week of April, and she did not mention it again.

. . .

When a family of smiling gypsies appeared in the stable yard, Frau Schmidt flung open a kitchen window and screamed, *"Raus, ihr Schweine, oder ich lasse euch verprügeln!"* Get out, you swine, or I'll have you thrashed! The gypsies did not bother to answer or even to look at her, sauntering down the avenue, followed by Felix's dogs.

When I saw that one of the boys carried Bessie, Felix's favorite brown-and-white spaniel, I put down my work and rushed after them. When the boy saw me, he gave a loud laugh and threw Bessie high into the air. She fell on the grass unharmed and I was able to grab her collar, but the excited dogs raced after the gypsies, ignoring my command to heel. When, a few minutes later, the dogs ran yelping into the yard, there were only two of them.

It was uncommon to see strangers at Löwendorf, but workers from Poland, many of them young and wearing the letter *P* on their clothes, had begun to appear in the village soon after the war began, headed for Ludwigsfelde and other nearby cities. The conscripted foreign workers, sent to work on the land when the farmers were mobilized, were tormented by the farmers' children, and the farmers' wives gave them only a portion of the meager rations allotted the workers by the government. Some of them soon escaped to find their way home, but others came to the Yellow Palace after dark for food. Felix instructed Kreck to give them cheese, bread, and beer. Fortunately there was enough for everyone. Cows had begun to disappear mysteriously from the village, and it was growing hard to find food. When Caspar came upon bits of hide from Felix's two prize Friesians, he lost his head, running across the park with the reeking skins in his hands. Alarmed by his cries, we rushed into the stable yard. "People are hungry," Felix said quietly as he led Caspar to the pump to wash his hands.

Soon after this, Felix asked Kreck how much food was held in reserve at Löwendorf. Along with their treasure, the Metzenburgs had brought champagne and wine, Turkish tobacco, gramophone records, and books from Berlin, but not much food, relying on the countryside to supply the needs of the estate. A levy of grain, meat, and poultry was by law sent each month to the army, with rapid and dire punishment for hoarding, resulting in a shortage of food, with inevitable speculation, even in a small village like Löwendorf. The quality of food was beginning to suffer (flour mixed with sawdust).

Kreck reported that we had stores of rice, potatoes, salt, dried fruit, cheese, flour, jam, and vegetables (not much coffee, sugar, or oil), and wine from the old baroness's cellar. There was enough animal fodder, as well as hay and oats to last to the next harvest.

The village women engaged by Dorothea as maids stopped coming to the house that spring, and the old men who worked as grooms and gardeners disappeared. I began to help in the kitchen and in the laundry, and Caspar and I worked in the garden. In Ballycarra, I'd swept the house, washed dishes, and made beds, but I was not used to working outside. I soon discovered that I preferred it to other work. As I bent to lift a basket of potatoes or reached to hang sheets on the line, I could feel the strength streaming through my arms and down my back, and it made me happy.

A certain amount of time was necessary to prepare dinner, given the numerous ways to cook and, what was perhaps more important, to present root vegetables. I learned from Schmidt six recipes for potatoes (which for an Irishwoman is something). Caspar's ferret caught rabbits, and I learned to skin and clean them. We bottled fruit from the orchard and hid the jars in the basement.

Roeder, who'd made it clear that any responsibility other than caring for Dorothea would be met with resentment, was soon worn down by the simple fact that she, too, required nourishment—I noticed that she was willing to perform any task deemed sufficiently refined for one in her position. Shelling peas fell into this category, as did watering the topiary on the terrace and making toast, although scouring pots, cleaning the stove, or washing sheets did not qualify. As she wore black lace gloves at all times, I had never seen her bare hands, and I still didn't see them.

Kreck tended the door, although there were no longer many visitors, and saw to the general running of the house, as well as serving at table with Caspar's assistance (Caspar, to Kreck's begrudging admiration, was a flawless servant). I offered to polish the parquet floors, which seemed only to require me to skate soundlessly through the rooms, arms clasped behind my back, feet wrapped in pieces of old carpet, but Kreck refused my help, perhaps because he liked to skate himself.

Kreck was also in charge of the ration books. Each citizen of the Reich was meant to receive seven ration cards a month, but the number of calories was continually reduced, the cards difficult to obtain and frequently unavailable. Blue was for meat; yellow for cheese, milk, and yoghurt; white for jam and sugar; green for eggs; orange for bread. Pink was for rice, cereal, flour, tea, and coffee substitutes. Purple was for sweets, nuts, and fruit. Seafood was impossible to find because of the mining of coastal waters and the war in the Atlantic. The coffee substitute, called nigger sweat, was made of roasted acorns, and we counted ourselves fortunate when Kreck could find it.

On the tenth of May, the Germans violated the neutrality of Holland, Belgium, and Luxembourg in a surprise attack led by the Tank Corps, with a view to invading France at its weakest point. On the thirteenth, as anticipated, the German army crossed the Meuse and entered France. In June, we heard the news that Italy had joined the war on the side of the Axis, which confirmed to some, although not to Felix, that the rapid defeat of England and France was imminent. Thousands of Jews who had managed to leave Germany were arrested and sent to work camps.

Not a week passed when something did not arrive from the Metzenburgs' friends in Berlin for Felix to hide. Silver teapots and rolled canvases were easily managed, but chairs and tables—even an organ on a wagon drawn by two weary horses—were more difficult (Felix sent the organ back to Berlin with his regrets). Kreck, convinced that we were surrounded by enemies, refused to hire boys from the village, and Caspar unloaded the treasure before wrapping it in canvas and packing it in metal-lined trunks. They were like actors on a stage, illuminated by lanterns, as Kreck would only allow Caspar to empty the wagons after dark, pacing and waving his arms (I once heard Kreck say, "This is a *very* inferior Rubens, my dear"). It soon became necessary for Felix to draw a map of the location of all the buried and hidden treasure, the Metzenburgs' as well as that of their friends, which he kept in his waistcoat pocket.

The summer was unusually hot, with frequent thunderstorms. Hundreds of redhead smews arrived on the river and I made sketches of them for Mr. Knox.

When I could find the time, I worked in the library, packing books. Shortly before tea, Kreck would arrive to change the blotting paper on the desks. The mother of Frau Metzenburg had been exiled to Löwendorf in 1919, according to Kreck, thanks to a careless maid who'd forgotten to change the paper. Herr Schumacher had held the compromising blotter to a mirror in order to read the letter his wife had written that morning to her lover, and Kreck did not want it to happen again. His mustache made him look as if he were always smiling, a deception that fooled me for some time, and I couldn't tell if he was teasing me.

I'd discovered that before coming to Löwendorf, Herr Elias had been a teacher at the Youth Aliyah School in Berlin, where he had prepared Jewish children for emigration to Palestine, teaching Hebrew and Zionist history. After Kristallnacht,

Felix, who'd met Herr Elias through a dealer in rare books, had arranged for him to leave Berlin to work in the library at Löwendorf. The village children, whose idea of a Jew was a man with horns, had quickly grown attached to Herr Elias, who lived in the village, perhaps because he played music for them on his gramophone and fed them.

I was surprised one evening by a small black bear in a ruffled skirt that had strolled away from some Hungarians busy stealing fruit in the orchard. Fortunately, she was tame, and when I turned to run, she did not chase me.

When I spoke to the Metzenburgs, I addressed them as Herr Felix and Frau Dorothea, but that summer they began to call me Maeve, rather than Miss Palmer. Felix preferred the company of as many people as possible, and I was occasionally asked to join them in the dining room. I wasn't asked if guests were expected, but visitors had become rare at Löwendorf. The Metzenburgs' isolation was difficult for Felix, accustomed as he was to brilliant conversation (or so I imagined), if not the distraction of sophisticated companions, but Dorothea did not seem to mind it at all. I seldom saw her. During the day, she drove to the village to visit the sick, taking them clothes and medicine, and to call on the old people who'd been left behind, often without food or money, when their sons and grandsons were sent to the front. I'd noticed that a house, a dog, a child, or even a crisis often enabled, if not compelled, people to remain together. It gave them, among other things, a subject. I was not the Metzenburgs' subject, but I provided an easy distraction for them while they learned to be alone. It was not my conversation that was sought, but my presence, which both inhibited and stimulated them.

I was a bit stiff at first, and always five minutes too early in the dining room, having raced to change my clothes after I helped Caspar and Schmidt to prepare dinner (the first night, I caught Dorothea staring at Inéz's black dress, trying to remember where she'd seen it before). It didn't take long for me to learn that it was considered bad luck to hand a saltcellar to someone rather than to place it before him, and that one did not say "God bless" at the start of a meal. If, for some reason, you had to leave the table, you did not do so without first asking to be excused. You did not drink tea with dinner, as did my mother. You did not use your napkin to wipe anything other than your mouth, as did my father. You did not eat with animals on your lap, as did some of the Metzenburgs' friends (I didn't count Mr. Knox and his gull, who always took tea with us).

The Metzenburgs kept to their vow not to speak at night about the war, talking instead about books and paintings, or the care of the estate—the weirs needed to be cleaned and the fields planted (there was no seed and no one to plant it), but most of the time they, too, were silent. When they spoke to friends on the telephone, they used a code, grinning slyly, that seemed alarmingly obvious to me—horses meant England, chickens meant Germany, peacocks meant France, bears meant Russia—but fortunately there seldom were telephone calls.

They often listened to the gramophone, perhaps a recording from 1936 of *Der Rosenkavalier*, or Karajan conducting Strauss.

When Dorothea said that Strauss wrote *Ein Heldenleben* (we were listening to it for the second night in a row) after a quarrel with his wife, the jarring notes reminiscent of his wife's voice, Felix asked her where in the world she heard such nonsense. He thought it very romantic of her to countenance everything that she heard. As he believed that things could be made perfect, which was to me the most romantic idea of all, his condescension seemed unjust. I waited for Dorothea's answer, but she was silent, bent over a book on Japanese moss gardens. "It was Strauss," Felix said as an afterthought, "who expressed his gratitude to the Führer for his interest in art." He paused. "It presents a conflict, of course, but there are greater ones."

Most nights, however, they listened to dance music. I looked forward to it, the songs going through my head all the following day. I was fond of the French heartthrob Jean Sablon, especially his song "Two Sleepy People." And Lys Gauty, whose song "La Chaland Qui Passe" made me sad (Felix noticed its effect on me and pointed out that it was a song about a barge). Felix preferred Adam Aston, particularly when he sang "Cocktails for Two" in Polish, and I wondered if it reminded him of a love affair, or two. Once, while listening to *The Threepenny Opera*, music banned by the Nazis, Felix and Dorothea rose with a smile at the start of "Wie Man Sich Bettet" and danced to it.

When it was time for the news, Dorothea preferred a program on Berlin radio called *Atlantis*. It was very popular, perhaps because it featured gossip about the Nazis, and it left her less frightened than the other broadcasts. There were frequent reports of Eva Braun's brother-in-law and of Reichsmarschall Göring, who liked to entertain foreign diplomats while wearing gold leather shorts, his toenails painted red. Felix said that the program clearly had many informants, as the scandal was often only a day or two old, and almost always accurate, which made me wonder how he knew.

It was after an evening of listening to music with Felix and Dorothea that I slipped the amber cigarette holder, the silver dish, the gloves, and the pen that I'd hidden in my room into a drawer of a desk in the library, keeping only Felix's batiste handkerchief.

Frau Schumacher had given Caspar a gift of an ordinary People's Radio with both an AM and a shortwave band, which he kept on a special table of its own in his room over the stables. Although people in Ludwigsfelde had been arrested for listening to prohibited radio stations, he was defiant in his devotion to the illegal broadcasts, and he invited me to listen to what he called the real news (as opposed to gossip) on those nights when he was able to find a station.

People had also been arrested for spreading rumors, traveling without permission, and dancing. A young woman in Blankenfelde had been imprisoned for falling in love with a Czech. All the same, I knew that I, too, would dance and fall in love were I given the chance, and I would certainly listen to forbidden broadcasts.

The gun room, its glass cabinets lined with green baize, was next to Caspar's room (the only guns were two antique rifles, their stocks inlaid with mother-of-pearl). Fishing gear was also kept in the room, and I often used the trout rods, their tips poking from monogrammed holland cases. Caspar found me there one night when he came to look for me—the broadcast from London had already begun—and as he closed the door behind us, said primly that women were customarily not allowed in the gun room.

It took several minutes for Caspar to arrange his room to his liking. He pulled a rush chair to the fire, then to the window, then back to the fire again. He placed a tray with a few walnuts and a pot of verbena tea next to the chair. On the nights when Herr Elias joined us, often arriving after midnight, there was wheat beer as well as tea. Herr Elias liked to sit on the narrow bed that once belonged to the footman. Caspar sprawled across his own bed, his long arms folded behind his head, his arms as white as milk where his sleeves fell away. I kept my eyes on the radio, but sometimes it was difficult. I'd been embarrassed at first to be alone with Caspar, having never before been alone with a man in his bedroom. Although the small room with its low ceiling seemed to encourage confidences, I could think of nothing to say. Soon enough, however, those things that had at first alarmed me—a chamber pot, only partially hidden under the bed, where he kept his slingshots and his collection of fossils, the bed itself, even his clogs—resumed their more prosaic significance, and I was able to listen to the news with composure. I could even have a conversation now and then.

There were many programs from which to choose, but Herr Elias preferred one called *Weltchronik*, broadcast from Switzerland every Friday by a Professor von Salis. One night as Caspar tirelessly manipulated the dials (the radio was old and often broke down, despite the short lengths of wire inserted through the back panel), he said that before his accident with the otter trap, his dream had been to be a fighter pilot. "Yes," said Herr Elias, lighting a cigarette from a straw held to the fire. "The Luftwaffe holds the last vestige of élan for us." At Caspar's look of interest, he said, "A word we learned in the Great War." Before Herr Elias could explain, the radio crackled into life, and we listened to a report of the bombing of London. I shakily poured them glasses of beer, but they did not want any. We listened late into the night, the men only leaving the room to visit the lavatory, which I, despite the tea, was still too embarrassed to do.

Sometimes I found Kreck in Caspar's room, polishing boots while they listened to the radio. They had become friends. I knew that Kreck often saved an egg or a potato for him, and I once found him clutching a sweater that Caspar had left in the library.

Caspar said that the strict laws against the mixing of races had been devised, in part, because the government feared that there was insufficient hatred of the enemy. On the contrary, Kreck said, huffing and puffing, there are at least two kinds of hatred—the lower classes blame the war on rich English lords, and the rich quite rightly blame the peasants of Russia.

In early June, we heard a broadcast on BBC by Winston Churchill, which began with the terrible words "The news from France is very bad. What has happened in France makes no difference to our actions and purpose. We have become the sole champions now in arms to defend the world cause. We shall do our best to be worthy of this high honor." I left my chair to sit with Caspar at the bottom of his bed, closer to the wireless. He was ashen, and Kreck had left the room.

A few days after Churchill's speech, Dorothea invited me to swim with her in the river. As I couldn't swim and didn't own a bathing suit, I told her that I'd be happy to accompany her, but that I couldn't go into the water, leading her to believe that I was menstruating, which was a little less shaming than not knowing how to swim.

As we walked across the park, she asked if I would make her an evening gown, perhaps in lace. I was surprised, as she had never shown an interest in lace, despite Inéz's claim. Although I now and then looked at my books of patterns, I myself had less interest than I once had—what had been romantic in Ballycarra seemed fussy at Löwendorf. What had once beguiled the long days no longer served to distract me. She said that it had been years since she'd had a new dress and she admired the lace dress I'd made for myself. I said that I'd be happy to make it for her. I had wondered why she'd asked me to go with her to the river and I had my answer.

I sat on the bank as she took off her robe. Her body was pale and straight, the bones protruding from her back like bleached twigs. She tucked her hair into a white rubber cap and slipped without a sound into the cold water. With her sleek white cap, black swimming goggles, and black bathing suit, she looked like a spectacled eider—I thought of the noisy tumbling of the

Irish girls as they splashed in the river in their summer dresses, the light cotton far more revealing than any swimming costume, and I felt homesick. As I watched her swim slowly across the river, her head turning stiffly from side to side, I heard someone call her name.

Roeder, out of breath, her hand on her heart, was stumbling across the park. She'd come to tell us that the Germans were in Paris.

Felix asked Caspar and Herr Elias if they would carry Frau Schumacher's harpsichord from the music room to the cellar. Most of the furniture, as well as the paintings and porcelain, had already been removed and buried in the park or hidden. There'd been so much treasure that many things had to be carried across the park to the Pavilion.

While the men measured the doorjamb, I sat at the harpsichord to play the one song that I knew, an air composed by Carolan for my ancestor Frank Palmer. Felix, having returned at the sound of the first tentative notes, unnaturally loud in the empty room, waited politely out of sight until I'd finished. "Well, it isn't Bach," he said, not unkindly, as I jumped to my feet.

It was soon determined, to Caspar's and Herr Elias's relief, that the door to the cellar was too narrow for the harpsichord, and the men had a glass of schnapps. As I was leaving, Herr Elias stopped me on the stairs to ask if I would mind helping him in the library. A number of Italian quartos in Felix's collection were going to the bank in Berlin, and he needed my help in packing them.

I followed him to the library, waiting as he removed the parchment folios from their calfskin folders. "I like it here," I heard myself say. "I mean in this room. And the very idea that it will take me twenty years to read every book." I realized that I sounded like Felix. It was the sort of thing that he might say. I would never read every book. I couldn't even read the titles.

I noticed an ink stain on his cuff. He smelled like peaches (the schnapps). He said that one of the manuscripts was *Lives of the Philosophers*, and the other, its frontispiece an engraving of a swan, its neck tied in a knot, was the *Decameron*. I wondered if the brush of his fingers as he handed me the folios was accidental, and I felt my face grow warm. He said that he had known that Felix owned the manuscripts, but given the war, he had never dreamed that he would see them. He'd forgotten to turn off the gramophone, and the record went round and round with a faint scratching sound. "Do you dance?" he asked suddenly.

I'd seen Felix and Dorothea dance, although not the fox-trot (when I'd read about the fox-trot in Ballycarra, I'd imagined that it required dainty mincing steps, curled hands held chest high, wrists limp—another of the many things I had wrong). He went to the gramophone to fit the needle into a groove. It was a recording of "Body and Soul" by Benny Goodman. He held out his hand.

Wiping my damp palms against my sides, I stepped (daintily, but without the raised paws) into the center of the room.

He placed my hand on his shoulder. He pressed his own hand against the small of my back and pulled me close.

I wasn't sure that he was familiar with the fox-trot himself. Our faces were so close that it was a relief to be able to stare into the distance, giving me, I fear, an exceedingly dreamy look. I *was* dreaming! Nothing had prepared me—certainly not my mild fantasies about Felix, which required the Rolls, cigarettes, and a gardenia corsage, or the nagging, itching curiosity I'd felt about the Catholic boys—for the combination of calm and hysteria that overcame me. I was afraid that he could hear the beating of my heart. As he moved me tentatively around the room, now and then bumping into a table, I could feel the most intimate parts of his body, creating in me a strange sensation of protectiveness and desire. For a moment, his mouth rested against the side of my face.

The music would soon end, and I forced myself to look at him. I knew that it was important to remember everything. I'd memorized the shape of his brow and moved on to his mouth—there were traces of charcoal between his teeth (no toothpaste)—when there was a sharp rap at the door. He stopped dancing, but he did not release me. I pulled away and went to the door.

It was Caspar. He peered around the half-opened door. "Frau Metzenburg sent me," he said.

Herr Elias appeared behind me. "Fräulein Palmer and I were dancing," he said. For an instant his hand was on my back again. For all that I had stared at him, I saw that he remained hidden, would always remain hidden, and I stepped aside to let him pass. He bowed slightly, smiling gently at Caspar as he pushed past us into the room, looked around wildly, and then ran out. Herr Elias closed the door and played the song again.

A few days later, Caspar found me in the kitchen garden to tell me that Herr Elias lived with a woman in the village. I said nothing but continued with my weeding. He also told me that Germany had invaded Romania. He sat cross-legged on the sandy path and began to cry.

He said that his sister, who'd once been as fat as butter, had been arrested in May and taken to Sachsenhausen for the crime of racial defilement. As the lover of a Frenchman, she'd been sentenced to three years of hard labor. She'd been chosen at random to work in a dye factory, where the workers were suffering from chemical poisoning. She had already lost her sense of smell, and she had difficulty breathing. The dyers were like diseased birds, their eyes inflamed and their skin covered with scales.

I gave him my handkerchief. He wiped his face and then placed the handkerchief on his thigh, smoothing it with his hands. Some of the lace bridges had torn, and he pieced them together before folding it into a square. I reached to take it from him, but he slipped it into his pocket. I gave him a basket of tomatoes to take into the house and went back to my weeding.

British bombers on their way to Berlin flew over Löwendorf for the first time that summer. There were hundreds of them, and the steady drone of their engines shook the windows and doors of the Yellow Palace. As soon as one wave was gone, another would arrive—it sometimes took two hours until the last of the planes passed overhead.

One moonless night when Felix was in Berlin, the sound of the bombers so frightened me that I felt my way down the stairs and ran from the darkened house to the stables, where I knew Caspar would be calming the horses. Dorothea was there, too, standing next to her hunter, Cloonturk, her hand on his quivering neck.

There was a smell of dry sacking and liniment as Caspar walked a horse back and forth in the dark. "The English usually fly by day," he said to the horse. "Their radar isn't very good, as I've told you, although it hardly matters. Their pilots are *kings*."

"They are on their way to Berlin," Dorothea said to me.

"They prefer a summer night like this, when the days are long and the skies are clear. But summer is almost over," Caspar said, sounding disappointed.

Dorothea and Caspar went from stall to stall, quieting the horses and the whining dogs, and I followed them. When Dorothea noticed that I was trembling, she put her scarf around my shoulders.

That Christmas, we heard the news that wild animals had escaped from the Berlin zoo during an RAF bombing. Crocodiles, snakes, and Siberian wolves were said to be hiding in every stairwell and hedge. A tiger strolled one morning into the Café Josty on Potsdamer Platz, where he devoured a Bienenstich cake and immediately died. One of the customers insinuated that it was the fault of the confectioner, and the café sued for slander. The court ordered that an autopsy be conducted. When pieces of glass were found in the tiger's stomach, the case was dismissed. We believed these stories because they eased our terror.

1941

It was bitterly cold in the new year, and Felix ordered that the gates to Löwendorf be left open at night so that strangers, whether escaped workers or refugees or even German soldiers, could be given cider and bread and a warm place to rest for the night—there were sometimes twenty people sleeping in the stables. Felix did not hold the soldiers responsible for the war. He often spoke to them and even wrote letters for them, which he arranged to be sent to their families. A young Dutch worker whose chest had been crushed by a cart was brought to the Yellow Palace, but we did not have the medicine or the skill to help him, and he died the next day. When Caspar buried him in the meadow, Kreck said, "*That,* I trust, is not going on Herr Felix's treasure map."

While working alone in the library one morning, I came upon a receipt tucked into an old photograph album of the old baroness and a woman companion on the Nile. The receipt, written to Felix Metzenburg, had a list of numbered items with the amounts paid for them. The figures were quite high, and I wondered if he'd been buying more treasure. I meant to give the receipt to him, but I forgot. He'd been feeling very low after hearing from Count von Arnstadt that Professor Wasselmann had been executed as a spy at Flossenbürg (I'd kept the note that I found at Christmas lunch, but when I heard the news, I burned it). Dorothea tried to comfort him by reminding him that it might be a rumor, but he said that he knew that it was true. He asked to see my passport in order to make certain that it was in order. I told him that Inéz had never returned it to me, and he nodded as if to say, Of course, she didn't return it. I made a note in my journal to ask her for it when I saw her.

I also found a collection of old *Jugend* magazines. There were beautiful women on the covers and more women inside, frequently entangled with animals—snakes but also sea lions, horses, and giraffes, although birds, especially those with long beaks, were given special favor. I was shocked at first, not knowing that such things were possible, and then less and less shocked and more and more intrigued. I could feel myself grow warm as I looked at the pictures, and later I wondered if such practices were known to Mr. Knox and what he thought of naked women cavorting with storks. I knew about Leda and the swan, of course, but it had never occurred to me that it wasn't a metaphor. Looking at the pictures, I realized that it was both a metaphor *and* real, and this discovery was thrilling to me. I sometimes took the magazines to my room.

Shortly before my birthday, I received a letter from Mr. Knox, dated 10 January 1941.

My dear Maeve, I would not be Irish did I not begin my letter with a remark on the weather, even though it is just as you remember, winter in Ballycarra being unfailingly damp and drear.

I asked Peter's brother, a new student, to look after Wedgwood when I was away, but the Catholic boys threw stones at them, and Peter's brother threw stones back at them, ending our arrangement.

Last October, my cousin, Clive Knox, was a crew member on an RAF bomber that overshot its base returning from an air raid on Berlin—I trust that you are still at Löwendorf, as it would be distressing to think that my cousin is bombing you—and was forced to ditch in the Irish Sea. He and his crew were, I'm delighted to report, rescued by a trawler from Waterford.

I wondered if Mr. Knox had written his letter late at night, perhaps after finishing the week's sermon. I imagined him at his neat desk, an oil lamp lighting the pages spread before him. He would have his pipe, and perhaps a glass of porter. He wrote that he was keeping busy with his research on the occurrence of infidelity in swallows and chickadees. He had observed over the years that when there was much rain and some fruit, the female tended to seek a male with the short bill best-suited to eating seeds, regardless of any previous commitment. *You might consider,* he wrote in closing, *learning the calls of certain birds—cuckoos, green pigeons, moorhens, and quails (as well as bees), to put to use when someday you marry.* He'd read this tip, as he called it, in Burton's translation of *The Thousand and One Nights.* He added in a postscript that he'd found no one who could read to him with my particular gifts of curiosity, innocence, and cupidity. A compliment, I decided. Although I often wrote about the Metzenburgs, he never mentioned them.

There was something new in his tone. He no longer addressed me as a girl, but as a young woman. I was flattered, of course, but also uneasy, as if I'd been given praise that I didn't deserve. When Inéz spoke to me in a knowing way, I was flattered (it was one of the reasons I so quickly agreed to go with her to Berlin), but it was different with Mr. Knox. It never occurred to me that his new tone might have something to do with my own letters.

Late one night, Roeder knocked on my door to ask if I would read to Frau Metzenburg. One of Dorothea's childhood friends had disappeared during the invasion of Yugoslavia. She'd written and telephoned her acquaintances in the Ministry and had gone twice to Berlin to spend the night in the small flat she kept, but her friend had not been found. She'd been unable to sleep since, and I often heard her walking through the house at night.

I was already in bed, but I told Roeder that I would go at

once. My room was cold, and I dressed quickly. I'd been tatting a snood for Dorothea, not unlike the one that Maria Milde had worn to Christmas lunch. Dorothea's hair had not been cut in two years. As Felix did not like things to lose their freshness, including people, I thought that she might find the snood useful. I'd used the last of my silk thread, and I sewed with the strands of horsehair that Caspar collected for me. I'd been working on her lace dress, but I was so unused to making lace that my hands tired quickly, and I'd had to put it aside.

I could speak a plain German, thanks to patient Herr Elias, but it was still easier for me to read it than to struggle for the right word. I'd been reading Flaubert to her in a German translation, as well as the diaries of Edmond de Goncourt, despite the occasional references to Jews and Jewesses. She'd scolded me for skipping a line in *Bouvard and Pécuchet* (*They all have hooked noses, exceptional minds, and servile souls that think of nothing but making money*), and I no longer omitted a word.

She was sitting in bed. Despite the fire, her room was as cold as my own room. The walls were covered in raw silk painted to resemble a forest. French doors opened onto the park, and mirrors were arranged so that the trees were reflected in them (in the morning, in the light, she appeared to be floating over a wood). On one wall was a large painting reaching from floor to ceiling of her mother in a red gown. The chimneypiece was painted with trompe l'oeil vines that climbed the wall and snaked across the ceiling. There was an alabaster lamp on either side of the ivory bed.

I pulled a chair to the bed and found my place in the book. The light from the fire gathered itself on the page, and I began to read. *One morning in the terrible winter of 1837, when she had put him in front of the fire because of the cold she found him dead in the middle of his cage, hanging head down with his claws caught in the bars. He had probably died of a stroke, but she thought he had been poisoned with parsley, and despite the absence of proof, her suspicions fell on Fanu. She wept so much that her mistress said to her, "Why don't you have him stuffed?"*

Pausing for breath, I saw that she'd fallen asleep. I closed the book and tiptoed across the room. As I reached the door, I heard her voice. Like most people who are reserved, she was intimidating, and I was always startled when she deigned to speak to me. Part of her fascination, of course, was her secretiveness. She could not bear to be anticipated, or forestalled, taking great care to conceal a meaningless or innocent gesture, with the inevitable result that we were obsessed with her every movement. Although she had no fear, she was as wary as a mouse.

"Perhaps you don't know that my mother went mad." She was under the covers, the quilt pulled to her chin. Her slanting hazel eyes, set far apart in her pale face, looked yellow in the light. The hair on either side of her center part was lifted into two small peaks, reminding me of a scops-owl with its feathered horns. With the painted walls and the smell of burning juniper boughs, I felt as if I were lost in a forest. "Last summer in Vienna," she said, "they rounded up all of the people walking in the Prater. The Jews were separated from the others, and they were ordered to remove their clothes. The men were made to crawl on all fours in the grass. Ladders were provided so that the women could sit naked on the branches of the trees, where they were made to sing like birds."

I was silent. I wondered in my confusion what kind of birds.

"Do you believe that story?" she asked, clutching the top of the quilt, the tips of her fingers like talons.

"I would like not to believe it."

"Far worse things are done every day."

"I'd prefer not to believe it."

"There is a certificate that acquits me of all tainted blood. I wouldn't believe that, either, if I were you."

"No."

"Good night then."

"Good night." I could hear her voice as I hurried down the passage, and I wondered if she was talking to her mother.

The spring was unusually cool, with rain nearly every day. We lived in a state of dampness, coughing and sneezing from morning till night. Toward the end of April, Countess Inéz, or, rather, the Princess Alkari, arrived from Cairo, where her husband served as secretary to his uncle, King Farouk. The prince had beauty and charm, but no money, and Inéz had volunteered to act as courier for Farouk as her nationality allowed her to travel more freely than others. She said that no one wanted Farouk himself, as he was known to steal everything in sight. Although Inéz could not bear the sight of anyone fat, she'd made an exception of the king.

To our joy, the royal dispatch bag was packed with dates,

salt fish, barley, olive oil, lemons, figs, and fava beans. Kreck called Inéz "our beauty of humble and tropical origin" when he carried the plates into the kitchen after lunch, and I realized that he was drunk.

Roeder found a small wooden box of rosewater jellies, dusted with powdered sugar, when she unpacked the princess's bags and, for a moment, thought that it was a present for her. "Her Highness seems to have a weakness for seamstresses," she said upon discovering my name on the card.

"I'm not a seamstress," I said.

"But *her* mother was a seamstress," Roeder said as she staggered under a pile of the princess's furs.

It had been months since I'd seen Inéz. I no longer wore my hair in a plait, having cut it myself after coming across a photograph of Louise Brooks in *Pandora's Box*. At dinner, I wore the black dress she'd given me, and for the first time, she complimented me on my chic. I was thrilled, of course, especially as I'd anticipated wearing the dress for her. Although Dorothea always looked smart in her navy suit (cashmere or raw silk, depending on the season), she didn't have Inéz's dash. Inéz had arrived at Löwendorf in her husband's red felt fez, and a golden sable coat, which, I suspected, did not come from the prince.

During a walk along the river, she again urged Dorothea to leave Germany. "It's not too late to dig up your treasure," she said in irritation, "if that's what keeps you from leaving."

"No, it's not the treasure that keeps us," Dorothea answered quietly. "Felix says they have no reason to mistrust us. That they haven't bothered us shows how little we concern them."

They were no longer guarded in their talk when I was with them—the prince's impotence, the ugly new hats, Don Jaime's gift to Inéz of an emerald necklace and a Titian (Felix said that Don Jaime gave it to her because Hitler had said in a speech that not everyone was in a position to buy a Titian). Their conversation seemed to distract them from the graver matters that troubled them.

Dorothea's favorite cousin, a major in the Luftwaffe, had been shot down over Belgrade during Operation Punishment. Inéz's former husband, Count Hartenfels, was a colonel in the Wehrmacht. Her distraction may have accounted for her vagueness when I told her that I needed my passport. Felix had been pressing me for it (and, I suspect, pressing her as well), and she promised to bring it with her on her next visit to Löwendorf.

That night, I ate all of the jellies in bed, one after another, my teeth glued together, unable to stop myself.

There were rumors that Hitler's deputy, Rudolf Hess, had flown a Messerschmitt across the Channel to Scotland in hope of negotiating a peace treaty with the Duke of Hamilton. Swiss radio reported that Hess had assumed that the British would be better disposed to Germany after Hitler's surprising decision to allow the British Army to escape at Dunkirk. The German news reports about Hess were very brief, and the BBC said nothing at all. In Ludwigsfelde, Caspar found leaflets that read *Deranged brown budgie mysteriously escaped from locked cage. If found, return immediately to Führer.*

.   .   .

Felix was called unexpectedly to Berlin, and Dorothea, who had been walking in the park, decided that dinner would be served on the roof of the temple, under the black-and-white striped awning. She sent Caspar to the village to ask Herr Elias to join us, and told Kreck to arrange everything for our arrival at dusk. Schmidt was making vichyssoise, a salad of wild greens, and a fruit compote. Dorothea told Kreck that he would not be needed once he'd set the table and brought the food. She would do the serving herself.

Dorothea's mother had grown honeysuckle on the roof in big earthenware pots, and the overgrown vines climbed the tent posts and across the awning. There was a rustic wicker table and two chaises with cushions, as well as comfortable chairs. The roof terrace did not really suit the austere little temple, and Kreck attributed this to Frau Schumacher's lack of refinement. There was a small high-ceilinged room on the ground floor where garden furniture and boating equipment were stored in the winter, with a narrow and dark staircase leading to the roof.

When we arrived, Kreck had done his work. The table was set, and there were candles and a bowl of white peonies. Herr Elias was on one of the chaises, looking as if Kreck had arranged him, too. He wore a pale linen suit with white canvas shoes. His Panama hat rested at the foot of the chaise. He was a bit of a dandy, I realized, and I found myself grateful that he did not lounge against the cushions, but sat with his legs hanging over the side, smoking a cigarette. Just as there are all kinds of strangeness, there are all kinds of seduction.

Dorothea blushed when she saw him. Kreck was busy with a

hamper of food, and she asked him to open a bottle of champagne. She moved restlessly around the table, arranging the silver and refolding the napkins. When she saw that Kreck had no intention of leaving, she sent him to the house for some salt. She asked me to take the peonies away, perhaps downstairs, as their smell was too strong. Banishing the peonies was something that Felix might have done, and I was surprised. When I returned, having struggled with the heavy bowl on the stairs, I heard Herr Elias say, "You're distracted tonight." His fingers encircled her wrist.

"I don't believe in distraction," she said, pulling away from him. "It's a way to be innocent and guilty at the same time."

"I find it useful," he said.

The sun had fallen behind the Night Wood, but she did not light the candles, knowing, as she would, that there was more beauty in the growing darkness. A smell of wet leaves rose from the park. I heard the loud hiss of a moorhen, threatened by a river rat perhaps. Bees, heavy with pollen, emerged reluctantly from the honeysuckle, staggering in their flight, and I reminded myself not to drink too much champagne. I sometimes had too much wine when I was ill at ease, and Dorothea and Herr Elias had unsettled me. He spoke to her in a low voice, and I turned away so as not to watch them. I wished that I could tell them that it was all right, that there was not enough love to go around as it was, but I suspected that they knew that.

There was a sound on the stairs. The top of Kreck's head appeared, and then his mustache. He had the salt, and some walnuts collected by Caspar in the woods. *"Ein besonderer Leckerbissen,"* he said. A special treat.

Dorothea took the tray from Kreck's hands. "Perhaps we should eat," she said with a sigh. "Kreck has gone to such trouble."

Herr Elias came to the table as Kreck poured the soup into bowls with a silver ladle. Dorothea sat next to me. Her hands were shaking and she put them in her lap. I thought about the fineness of suggestion, and the way that truth can be conveyed by a stray gesture, or even a sound. Of course, hints tend to contain too much, at least for me, but I managed to calm myself. Nothing had changed. What was worse, at least for them, nothing *would* change.

Dorothea asked if I would like a pear with my soup—we had abandoned certain conventions in regard to food—and when I said that I would, Kreck moved around the table to hold the dish at my side (we had not abandoned certain formalities). When I looked up from my soup, I saw that Herr Elias was watching me. His face, as always, was guarded, but still it was melancholy. He smiled hesitantly at me. It was a way to start again, I knew, and I smiled, too. The soup was delicious.

As Kreck seldom came to the second floor during the day, I knew as soon as I heard his shambling step that something bad had happened.

He'd come to tell me that Germany, breaking its pact with the Soviets, had invaded Russia. The few men and women under the age of sixty who had managed to remain in the village had been mobilized overnight, while others had been forcibly conscripted to work in factories in the newly conquered territories. He had hidden Caspar in a linen closet for the day.

With the swift capture of Minsk and Smolensk, Germany grew even more confident of victory. There was much talk of the Reich's secret weapon, which would soon be used to destroy London.

One evening in July, Dorothea asked me to walk with her to the clearing at the center of the Night Wood. The paths were made of softened dirt, but there'd been no gardeners in some time, and the way was scarcely visible beneath drifts of leaves and fallen branches. The trees, some of which had been trained to meet overhead, hadn't been trimmed, and the path was narrow.

Her grandfather had made the wood, planting maritime pines from Canada, Japanese larch, and silver firs from the Alps, as well as weeping birch, linden, yew, elder, oak, and ash so that the effect of pine would not be too overwhelming. He claimed that the smell of the Night Wood intoxicated him (less expensive than ether, said Felix), and in fine weather he had a camp bed carried to the clearing to watch the changing sky through the night.

The many paths were intended to be confusing, only one of them leading to the clearing at the center. "North, then west, south, and east, before proceeding in the reverse." She paused to make sure that I was listening. I memorized each turning (a rook's nest, a stand of ghost bramble, an oak split by lightning). Caspar had told me that he sometimes found bones in the woods that were not the bones of foxes or badgers, and Werewolves—the villagers' name for escaped criminals and lunatics—had recently been seen by the bridge. As we walked, I glanced nervously over my shoulder. The sky darkened, and the air grew heavy as the trees disappeared into the blackness.

The clearing was bright and fresh after the gloom of the forest. Japanese moss grew in tiny hillocks, soft to the foot. It began to rain, the drops sharp and cool on my face. When we left, Dorothea made me lead to make certain that I knew the way.

Felix asked Caspar to bury a painting by Cranach that he kept in his bedroom (the last thing he sees at night, I heard Dorothea say), but he changed his mind and told Caspar to hide it instead in the cellar of the Pavilion, where he could at least look at it now and then. As Dorothea did not consider any cellar to be a good hiding place, she had Caspar bury the Meissen turkey cock and pheasants and a necklace of yellow diamonds that had belonged to the Empress Josephine in the park.

The horses were requisitioned that summer by two German officers whose jeep broke down outside the gates. They harnessed Felix's hunters to an old victoria they found in the garage, tied the other horses to the back, one of them Dorothea's horse, Cloonturk, and drove away at a trot, the harness jingling loudly.

Once I'd finished packing Felix's books, Dorothea asked me to help her sort through her mother's papers and photographs.

"Have you noticed," she said, looking at a picture of her father, "that the simplest of good-byes now fills you with despair? Each time that Kreck leaves for the village, I'm certain that I will never see him again. I worry when Felix goes for a walk, unsure if he'll return. When Herr Elias does not appear for two days, I'm sure that he's been arrested. And such remorse! To be reminded, day after day, of all that hasn't been said or done."

"Is there something you wish to say now?" I asked, teasing her a little.

She frowned. "I've never thought that one should say everything. Even now."

I nodded, aware that I had been scolded, and we went back to work.

In the fall, Felix asked me to accompany him to Berlin as he wished to sell some treasure. He said that he preferred not to trouble Dorothea or Herr Elias, which I understood to mean that I was not to mention the purpose of our visit.

In the past, he'd sold his pictures through a friend in Amsterdam, the dealer Jacques Goudstikker, but the SS, he said, had broken Herr Goudstikker's neck as he tried to leave Holland. As Reichsmarschall Göring had promptly confiscated Herr Goudstikker's collection, Felix thought it safe to assume that Göring owned many of Felix's former paintings. After the fall of France, Göring had made twenty visits to the Jeu de Paume to choose art for his private museum, so his paintings, Felix said, were in excellent company. As it was forbidden to remove objects of cultural or artistic value from the city without permission from the Institute of Culture, which refused to give it, I nervously wondered if it was permissible to bring objects into the city. I'd begun to notice that when I was overwhelmed by the big things—Goudstikker, Göring—I permitted myself to worry about the small things. I said that I would be happy to help him.

On the train to town, Felix put aside his book and turned to me with an unaccustomed gravity, further unnerving me. He said that in conversations with friends still in the Foreign Office and in listening to the BBC, it had become apparent that Ireland was less neutral than she pretended to be. "Militant nationalists clearly hope to take advantage of England's engagement in a European war to reclaim the six Ulster counties, but this somewhat unrealistic plan is already collapsing. It doesn't help, of course, that the chief of staff of the Irish Republican Army was killed in a U-boat off the Irish coast. Did you know," he asked, "that RAF bombers returning from North Africa are permitted to refuel at Shannon?"

"Enraging the Führer, who had counted on a bit more help from us Irish."

He looked at me quizzically, and returned to his book.

In Berlin, he took my umbrella (the treasure, which I assumed was paintings, was inside both our umbrellas), suggesting that I spend an hour or two at the Ufa-Palast cinema before meeting him at the corner of Französische Strasse and Glinkastrasse. He needed a few hours, as he was hoping to see his tailor once his business was finished. I did as he said and went to the cinema, where I watched a newsreel in which Maréchal

Pétain asked his countrymen to honor France by volunteering as foreign workers—a man could earn top wages, as well as the release of a French prisoner of war (four workers for one prisoner). There was also a report encouraging Frenchwomen to cut their hair and send it to the government, as hair was needed to make clothes. I was not so sure about the high wages for foreign workers. The workers who'd been sent to the countryside around Löwendorf earned no wages at all. A new film, *Hab Mich Lieb*, starring Marika Rökk, followed the newsreel. In the finale, Fräulein Rökk rips away her gown of white feathers at the distant sound of a jazz band to reveal a spangled bolero and a tiny pair of shorts. I wondered what the Nazis were trying to tell me (I'd thought that swing music was banned). The film so disturbed me that I was incapable of leaving my seat when it ended.

I was late for my rendezvous with Felix. As I hurried along (it was difficult to walk in Inéz's alligator shoes, two sizes too big), I noticed that the once-familiar Jewish shops and businesses had Aryan names. Although the passersby behaved as if nothing in Berlin had changed, I saw several well-dressed women scavenging for food in trash bins and signs prohibiting Jews from buying newspapers or sitting in gardens after dark.

Felix was waiting for me on the corner, smoking a cigarette as he glanced at the morning's paper. The train to Löwendorf would not leave for three hours, he said, and he wondered if I would mind if we had a late lunch at the Hotel Adlon, which was nearby. Just the sight of him lifted my mood, and I was amused, as I often was, by his thinking or at least pretending that I had the choice of refusing him. One would have thought that having my company was the one thing lacking in his life.

As we walked the short distance to the hotel, he explained that the Ministry of Defense had built two special air-raid shelters at the Adlon at Hitler's order to ensure the safety of the foreign delegations who were the hotel's patrons, as well as party members whose offices were in nearby Wilhelmstrasse. The shelters had been rather like first- and third-class compartments on a train. "The original shelter for hotel guests was a square plaster box only five yards underground, while a vast shelter deep in the earth with running water, private rooms, and a loudspeaker system was reserved for more important visitors, who were awarded special pink tickets. Those unfortunate enough to be directed to the first shelter protested with such fury that soon everyone was admitted to the superior shelter, with or without a ticket. The first shelter is now used to store abandoned suitcases."

Herr Adlon rushed from the dining room when he saw Felix, guiding us smoothly past the crowd of men and women noisily waving cartons of cigarettes in the hope of obtaining a table or at least a room upstairs. Felix waited (I noticed that he was one of the few people who did not glance ceaselessly around the room) while Herr Adlon, smiling as if he had the pleasure of seeing me every afternoon and again in the evening, pulled out my chair (I saw that he knew *not* to kiss my hand). "No morels today, Herr Metzenburg," he said mournfully as he lit Felix's cigarette, nodding to an elderly waiter with a magnum of wine. He took our coats with a wink, promising to look after them. Felix ordered our lunch (caviar with toast, an omelet, endive salad, and champagne). I opened my napkin and spread it neatly across my lap.

I was unused to eating in restaurants, and I watched him closely. I was relieved to be wearing Inéz's gray suit and lavender gloves—I could see that people were looking at me, but only because I was with Felix. He, too, was staring at me or, rather, staring at Inéz's suit. "You're looking very well today," he said.

The other women in the room wore the new short skirts, some made from curtain material, with shoes cut from cork, and jersey turbans (no shampoo). The men were in dark double-breasted suits, their hats placed next to them on the tables, their coats on the backs of their chairs, and a few were in uniform (Kreck said that it was vulgar to wear your uniform on private occasions). People were staring at a small dark-haired woman who sat with a man wearing a Nazi armband. She wore neither a turban nor a chintz skirt but a tweed coat flecked with metallic thread and a beret stuck with several brooches. Felix noticed that I, too, was staring at her. "Mademoiselle Chanel," he said, "and her protector, Baron von Din-klage." Felix caught the eye of the baron, and they nodded to each other. I was shocked, having not yet understood that it was possible to make beautiful things even if you were corrupt, unlike the Irish lace makers in Ballycarra, who made beautiful things and were only thought to be corrupt. I knew of Mademoiselle Chanel, of course—she and Inéz were old friends.

"Did you notice, by any chance, that Holbein of a goldsmith in the window of the auction house?" Felix asked. "That is where Dorothea found the little Nicholas Hilliard she gave me for my birthday."

"Yes," I said. "Suitable for hiding."

To my delight, he smiled. "I can think of nothing else. It's rather like seeing a woman you desire. Perhaps better. Of course, it belongs to the Czernins. I'm thinking of buying it." He lifted himself from his chair to greet two friends, men who, unlike the others, did not look as if they were on a stage. They didn't look as if they belonged there, either, despite their natural air of privilege. Of course, it was these men who'd once had the dining room of the Adlon to themselves. Their tense grace barely concealed their rage.

I found it difficult to look at people, fearful of what more I might see. Was the girl with the frowning Oberstleutnant a collaborator? Did she hide Jews in her attic? Did the man in the chalk-striped suit use Polish slaves in his factories? Did that woman sell gold on the black market? Passports? Art stolen from Jews? Felix had told me that in Hamburg the daily auctions of the confiscated possessions of Jewish citizens were so crowded that it was standing room only. No one was who he appeared to be—it was too dangerous to be yourself, unless you were one of them, and perhaps even then. Even I was pretending to be someone else, at least for the afternoon.

Felix caught sight of Count von Arnstadt, standing in the doorway to the dining room, and nodded to him. My heart sank. I wanted to be alone with Felix, people staring at us as we toasted each other with champagne (even if Felix didn't toast).

"In the beginning," Felix said, smiling at a woman in a heavy mink coat (people no longer left their coats with an attendant, as they were certain to be stolen) whose gloved hand Arnstadt was bending to kiss, "my friends said, 'Oh, come now, *mon vieux*, it's not quite so bad as you feared,' but in a very few weeks, they all said, 'Nothing could be as hellish as this. What were we thinking?' " He was silent, looking both contemptuous and amused. "We once found it humorous to buy those postcards sold at newspaper kiosks—perhaps you've seen them or even sent one yourself—Göring in a fur hat and cowboy boots or the Führer looking apoplectic."

Arnstadt at last reached our table, a mocking smile in readiness for Felix. "The Adlon is full of beautiful women today," he said as he sat down.

"They can't *all* be Poles," said Felix.

"And Helldorf with three of the loveliest. Of course, he is the richest man in Berlin. Thanks to the extremely lucrative market in passports."

Felix opened his mouth to speak, then closed it as he caught sight of Baron von Dinklage coming toward us. At Felix's expression, the baron turned into the lobby—Felix's combination of decadence and rectitude made him difficult to read, but the baron seemed to have no trouble at all.

"*Sie haben Glück gehabt bisher, Felix,*" said Arnstadt. "*All die Jahre hatte ich keine Ahnung, dass Sie so ein Spieler sind.*" You've had luck so far. All these years, I had no idea you were such a gambler.

Felix frowned in irritation and turned to me. "*Maeve, du hast deinen Sekt gar nicht getrunken.*" It was not so much my thirst that concerned him, as his wish to warn the count that I understood German. He was silent as the waiter filled his glass with champagne. "I hope that you'll have lunch with us," he said to Arnstadt when the waiter was gone. "Thanks to the precautions taken by our Führer, it is the place where we are least likely to die."

"Unfortunately, today is the day I deliver the Little Friend to the Chancellery." He paused to light a cigarette. "You may be interested to know that our friends' affairs are less Feydeau than we like to imagine."

"*Quite* interested," Felix said.

Arnstadt looked at his watch. "We banned Helen Keller today." Sensing my confusion, he gave me a smile that could only be called sinister.

"Stop teasing her," Felix said.

"Would that I were," said the count.

The melodic ring of a gong, more like a dinner bell than an alarm, sent a surge of fear through the room. It was the signal for guests, waiters, bellboys, cooks, and Herr Adlon himself to race for the stairs. We went down a narrow, harshly lit staircase, Felix's hand not quite touching the small of my back, and found ourselves with sixty people in a large whitewashed room with rows of wooden benches, much like a country schoolroom. Arnstadt had disappeared. I saw Mademoiselle Chanel and her baron ushered into a private room.

Felix made a place for me on a bench, regretting its roughness, and we sat down. It was much colder underground than in the dining room (we never saw our coats again). "I apologize," he said, "for the smell." I thought at first that he meant the smell of rotting potatoes, but he said, "When the ban against bathing more than twice a week was issued, it never occurred to me that some people were relieved."

There were men and women on the benches behind and in front of us, and in each of the other eight rooms, and the conversations were in many languages. The young man next to me, whom I'd noticed in the restaurant having lunch with a woman I took to be his grandmother, was reading a book by H. P. Lovecraft. The boy's grandmother was not with him, and I wondered if they'd been separated and if she was safe in another room. The waiters who had shoved their way down the stairs a few minutes earlier draped white cloths over their arms and held trays of pink gin cocktails at the end of each row.

The loudspeaker began to hum. A man's voice, in the tone he might use to read a child a story, said, "A number of horses from the riding stables in Tiergarten, their manes and tails on fire, are now racing up and down Kurfürstendamm," and several peopled laughed loudly. Men opened newspapers, women made lists with little gold pens, their handbags used for support, and some fell into a deep sleep, chins propped in their hands. Even Felix was quiet, and I was able to stare at him. I realized as I watched him how much I had come to trust him. With the vanity of a beloved man, he assumed that the doing and undoing of daily life (the smell of the unwashed, the lack of mushrooms, the uncomfortable benches) were, if not his responsibility, at least his to ameliorate, and I had come to expect it of him, too.

"The Chancellery is issuing new regulations concerning

domestic staff," he said, startling me. "You, Miss Palmer, will be required to sleep at least nine hours a day, and you will have one entirely free day as opposed to two free afternoons a week. Which means that today has been your free day."

I was sorry not to have a quick answer for him. His odd, sometimes irksome way of speaking as if he were an Edwardian lord still rattled me. A young woman sitting in the row in front of us had no such hesitation. Speaking English with a Viennese accent, she said in a voice just loud enough for us to hear, "Certainly wish *mine* would bring *me* to the Adlon on *my* day off." She turned her head to smile at us. Having already sized up our relationship from our conversation, she had not yet had actual sight of Felix, and when she did—his imperious, attractive, *rich* self—she liked what she saw. To my irritation, she swung around on the bench, not an easy thing to do, and sat facing us, her silky knees touching Felix's knees.

I did not look at him for fear that he liked it. I had an impulse to snag her stockings, but to my relief, the little bell rang to signify that the raid was over and that it was safe to return to the dining room. Felix helped the woman to her feet—she was a bit stiff after sitting in such a cramped space—steadying her with a hand on her elbow. Turning every few steps to make sure that we were behind him, he explained that he did not wish to see us survive an air raid only to be trampled by the French ambassador. It was Friday and the foreign diplomats would be rushing to the private dining room upstairs for their weekly lunch meeting with Ribbentrop. In the lobby, Felix kissed the woman's hand and said that had circumstances been less trying, he would have been pleased to accompany her wherever she was going. She kept her hand in his rather longer than I thought necessary. She did not say good-bye to me when she left to find her friends.

Felix watched her go and then turned to me with an amused smile. "Would you mind if we didn't stay for lunch?" he asked.

I said that I didn't mind at all (I'd been dreaming of the omelet). On the street, a disorderly company of shouting boys, members of Hitler Youth, was marching past, spades in hand, to the excited shouts of the crowd. Felix turned his back to them, the better to light his cigarette.

When I finished my chores, I sometimes took a book or my workbasket (and sometimes nothing at all) to the temple in the park, where I climbed to the roof to sit under the striped awning. I could see across the park to the Night Wood and beyond the river to the village.

As the Reich prohibited Jews from owning a sewing machine or typewriter unless it could be proved that it was a gift from an Aryan, Herr Felix had written a letter that Caspar delivered to the police station in Ludwigsfelde, stating that he, Felix von Metzenburg, had presented Herr Hector Elias with an Olivetti typewriter in 1937. I was curious to know what Kreck thought about this (we both knew it was a lie), but he said nothing, telling me a joke instead. "In the Great War, they used to say it would be over when officers had to eat the same food as soldiers. Now they say it will be over when Göring can fit into Goebbels's trousers." I realized that I'd never heard him laugh before.

·   ·   ·

America at last entered the war. Caspar and I huddled in his room, listening to the reports of the bombing of Pearl Harbor. The Japanese had sent nearly four hundred planes, flying in three waves, to bomb the Americans. Eighteen ships, including two battleships, had been lost, with three thousand dead. The Japanese had also attacked a hospital in Singapore, killing many of the doctors and a British corporal on an operating table. Hundreds of people, both staff and patients, many of them wounded, were marched to a warehouse where they were kept until morning, when the Japanese bayoneted them to death.

1942

There had been rumors all year about the murder of Jew-ish prisoners, but people continued to dismiss them. The villagers, and even some of the Metzenburgs' friends, said that while they had long and valuable friendships with one or two special Jews, the humiliation and misery inflicted on the country were in part the fault of the Jews, who had forgotten their place, lording it over the German people for far too long. Felix, when confronted with this commonplace (many Jews *were* Germans), answered that the madness that had overtaken Europe served to make us more alike, not less, but the villagers only smiled at him and shook their heads.

Felix said that he once believed that humanism had been

founded on the shared need to know. It had grown more and more apparent to him, however, that the opposite was true—we were united by our shared need not to know. "By the time that we understand what is happening," he said, "we are already complicit."

To the surprise of everyone, including Herr Elias, Felix decided to give a small lunch in Herr Elias's honor, choosing a day that fell in the same week as the Jewish feast of Passover. Dorothea asked him to reconsider the timing of the lunch, but he was insistent, irritably announcing that he would not succumb to intimidation. "No one is asking you to succumb to intimidation," she said; "rather, I want you to consider that you are putting your guests in danger." He refused to change his mind. The trees in the orchard were in bloom, and he told Kreck to fill the rooms of the Yellow Palace with branches of flowering plum and cherry. Caspar and I spent the morning on the river, fishing for brown trout with a footprint dun I found in the gun room.

I didn't know the story of Passover, and I'm not sure that anyone other than Herr Elias did, either. I'd asked Felix about it, and he read some of Exodus aloud to us at the table, much to the boredom of Inéz, who was spending two nights at Löwendorf on her way from Cairo to Paris. She sat next to Herr Elias, and I was on his other side. Next to Felix was Princess Bibesco, who was traveling with Inéz. Princess Bibesco wore a white silk dress embroidered with red roosters. Ropes of pearls were wrapped around her fingers and wrists, and on her head was a stiff crown of lace embroidered with a crest. (Inéz later told me that the princess had posed nude for the painter Boldini, something that Inéz herself had always hoped to do—he'd painted Inéz's portrait when she was sixteen, but unfortunately she'd been clothed.) If Inéz was bored and the princess opaque, Dorothea was enraged. She had again asked Felix to abandon his idea of a Passover lunch that morning, and he had again refused, rather grandly declaring that as horror was here to stay, she'd best get used to it. "Horror?" she'd repeated, over and over again, her voice barely audible.

Felix had placed three tins of his special blend of Turkish tobacco and some packets of cigarette paper at Herr Elias's place. The guest of honor was late, having walked from the village (Jews were forbidden to ride bicycles), a yellow star pinned unevenly to the left side of his tweed jacket. Felix greeted him affectionately. *"Ihr Stern ist unsere Schande,"* he said. Your star is our shame.

"Some people believe that a government that forbids certain of its citizens to possess toasters, irons, bicycles, or even a dog must feel unsure of its power, and this makes them careless," Dorothea said, her voice strained, but everyone ignored her.

The laws of the Reich forbade Jews to wear wool. They could not ride on trains or go to the theater, libraries, zoos, and parks. In Berlin, Jews could shop only between four and five in the afternoon, and they could not enter the district known as Judenbannbizirke, which stretched from Wilhelmstrasse to Unter den Linden. They were forbidden to drive or to use public telephones. They were not allowed in air-raid shelters. Herr Elias, despite wearing his star and giving up his bicycle, was breaking the law—his tweed jacket, his ginger cat, his gramophone.

We had a feast of wild asparagus, trout, warm potato salad, honey with the dried figs and dates brought by Inéz from Cairo, and many bottles of wine. When Felix apologized that there was no gefilte fish—he'd considered asking Schmidt to make it, but as it had never been served at Löwendorf and we were lacking many of the ingredients, he hadn't been confident of success—Inéz asked, "Gefilte fish? *Qu'est-ce que le poisson gefilte?*" I noticed that Herr Elias and Felix looked at each other for a moment, Herr Elias smiling slightly.

"*Mousse de poisson*," said Princess Bibesco.

"Ah," said Inéz. "*Comme une quenelle.*"

Inéz found me in the kitchen after lunch. "Do keep an eye on my friend, won't you? Only a child would refuse to save himself." I was cutting the figs to make jam, and she ate one, wiping her fingers on my apron. "And all because he cannot bear to leave his house or his Rembrandts."

"I don't believe he owns any Rembrandts," I said, offended on Felix's part.

"Don't be so sure," she said, turning to dazzle Schmidt with a smile. Frau Schmidt, unaccustomed to the presence of a princess in her kitchen, was rendered speechless, which was the point. "Remember, my dear," Inéz said to me, handing the last two bottles of Felix's Cheval Blanc to Frau Schmidt, who understood that she was to wrap them for the princess's journey, "that I myself am a *very* good example that there is always more treasure to be found." She took my passport from her handbag and dropped it into my pocket. "Let me know everything. The Egyptian ambassador will know where to find me." She did not tell me how I was to find the ambassador.

Dieter, the son of the innkeeper in the village, who drove Dorothea when she needed to go to Potsdam or Berlin, was taking the two princesses to the train station in one of Felix's cars. Dieter had not been mobilized thanks to a boating accident, but despite having only one arm, he was a good driver and mechanic. As he brought round the car, there was the sound of tires on gravel, and I heard Inéz say to Princess Bibesco, "Proper gravel at *last.*"

Later when I took the dogs to the stables, I heard what sounded like weeping. Felix was sitting on the terrace, his face wet with tears. "*Quenelle!*" he said when he saw me. "Her mother is a Jew." When he began to laugh, I realized that he wasn't offended by Inéz's pretense but admiring of her practicality and her audacity. He wiped his face with his handkerchief and gestured to me to sit with him. A smell of damp rose from the ground. He asked if I was chilly. He lit a cigarette.

I'd recently discovered (spying again) that he occasionally attended the secret meetings of an Italian Jesuit named Father Guardini, who lectured on philosophy. That spring, the priest had been discussing the *Duino Elegies.* I'd found a book of Rilke's poetry in the library at Löwendorf in which I came across the line *Poverty is a great radiance from within,* causing me to put aside the book.

Earlier that week, I'd followed Felix to the well where I knew he liked to hide treasure, watching from behind a wall as he pulled several packets from between the mossy stones, cursing in anger when he dropped one of them into the well. Two days later, three pots of honey, ten sacks of carrots, and a dozen baskets of potatoes mysteriously appeared in the Pavilion kitchen.

He put out his cigarette and said that he'd received an anonymous letter that his friend Bernhard Lichtenberg, the rector of St. Hedwig's Cathedral in Berlin, had been arrested for leading his congregation in prayers on behalf of the Jews and other prisoners in concentration camps. He'd learned, too, that a former neighbor in Fasanenstrasse, Frau von Schoon, had been sent to Ravensbrück with her two children. She'd been reported by an old servant for hiding the children's tutor, who was not only her lover, but Jewish. The tutor had been sent to Auschwitz. "At Ravensbrück," Felix said, "SS men in doctors' uniforms await new prisoners in the infirmary, where they are executed by a shot to the back of the neck as their height is measured. A recording of Richard Tauber singing 'Deis ist mein ganzes Herz' is played to cover the noise of the gunshots."

When we at last went inside, I found that Herr Elias had left me his copy of St. Augustine's *Confessions* with a note. *If you agree with Augustine that memory creates the self, then this is a book that will interest you, meine leibe—if, when this war is over, there remains a self to be created.* I'd told him, I'm afraid, that the German novels I'd been reading gave me unsettling dreams. I was a bit disappointed that his answer was to give me the book of an ascetic. That Augustine happened to ask God to defer his chastity to a later time was scant consolation.

·   ·   ·

The weather was mild through the spring, and Caspar was able to leave the window in his room open when we listened to the wireless. The sun, setting behind the park, gave the room a faint pink cast, and I often asked him to wait to the last moment before hanging the leather aprons he used as blackout curtains. The sky was filled with migrating geese—I thought I recognized the lesser white-fronted goose, but I couldn't be certain (Mr. Knox had taught me to be fastidious about identification). I no longer minded when my stomach made loud noises, and I regularly excused myself to go to the bathroom.

Caspar fussed with the wireless, using the two fingers of his right hand, while I mended a basket of Felix's hose. I had yet to finish Dorothea's evening gown. Although I took pleasure and even pride in my mending, I sometimes missed the sight of a *point de Venise* slowly taking shape in my hands.

We liked listening to Hilde Monte, who despised the Nazis and broadcast at great risk to herself, but one night, we heard instead the friendly voice of the American woman named Midge as she cheerfully reminded Allied soldiers that their wives and sweethearts were in bed with dirty Jews and Communists. Caspar, embarrassed, turned the dial to static. When I asked him about Midge, he said that the men in the village listened to her to keep Herr Pflüger from questioning their loyalty. When Reichsprotektor Heydrich was assassinated in Czechoslovakia, Herr Pflüger, the blacksmith's father and a party member, had felt it his responsibility to report those villagers he deemed insufficiently committed to Nazi ideals, and a guileless woman who worked as scullery maid at the inn had been taken away. Caspar was both impressed by Herr Pflüger and frightened by him. He said that until the end of the Great War, it had been impossible for a poor man to gain wealth and power in Germany, but with the rise of the Reich and the new opportunities for profit, it had become easier for men like Herr Pflüger to make their way. He said that someday those men would take over the world, and I wondered if he wished to be one of them.

After several minutes, he found a BBC report of the sinking of a German ship. He pared an apple as we listened, dropping pieces into my palm. Sometimes he lifted a slice to his mouth, holding it against the blade of the knife with his thumb. It was a relief to hear the educated English voice of the BBC broadcaster: "One by one, the Lancasters rolled in for the attack, the large ship easily visible on the clear, still water of the fjord. Accompanied by swift Soviet fighters, the bombers of the Royal Air Force deftly evaded the heavy armament bursting around them. The aerial assault was over in a matter of minutes. The Russian and English pilots watched in pride as the big ship capsized and disappeared into the black, icy water. More than twelve hundred Germans went down, singing 'Deutschland über alles.' " How the pilots knew that the sailors were singing troubled me, but I said nothing.

On a new station called the Calais Soldiers Broadcast, which was on the same wavelength as Radio Deutschland, we heard a report that rumors that the Nazis were murdering Jews in the camps might be true. The announcer (we'd grown adept at interpreting language and even the pronunciation and inflection of certain words) sounded as if he continued to find it incomprehensible, but Caspar believed the rumors. He said that some of the men in the village who were home on leave had been at Kiev, where they claimed to have seen and done terrible things. They had confided in their fathers and brothers, and the stories had been repeated in the village. "The truth," Caspar said, "will be worse than what we hear on the wireless. The truth will be worse than anything."

It was unusually hot that summer, and I spent as much time as possible on the river, even though Caspar scolded that it was no longer safe. He checked on me throughout the day and accompanied me to the bottom of the stairs when I went upstairs each night, waiting until Felix and Dorothea decided that it was time for bed.

He showed me a pistol and a box of shells he'd hidden in the gun room, giving me a quick lesson on how to load and fire it. As he returned the gun to its hiding place, he said that Kreck had recently traded a pair of silver brushes on Felix's behalf for tickets to a Furtwängler concert given by the Crown Princess Cecilie in Potsdam. "Not to be repeated," he said, "as Karajan and Furtwängler are enemies. Kreck says that if Maestro Karajan finds out, he will never speak to Herr Felix again." I promised not to tell a soul.

One morning in September, Roeder rushed into the sewing room to tell me that Herr Elias had been arrested, along with the miller and two foreign workers. I'd been sewing but had put my work aside to soak my hands in the tincture of raw alcohol and pine needles I used to ease the swelling in my fingers. To my dismay, my hands had begun to curl, as if I were hiding something in them.

I rode my bicycle to Herr Elias's house in the village, taking a shortcut through the fields. The door was open, and I ran inside. I'd often tried to imagine his rooms, and they were much as I'd pictured them. There was a gramophone and records and books, of course, and his typewriter, but also a pair of leather boxing gloves and a brown velvet dressing gown with a fringed sash. The drawers of his desk were open, but nothing seemed to have been touched. There were letters, and for a moment I was tempted to read them. Under the letters was his yellow star, the word JUDE smudged with ink. I found an embroidered handkerchief under a table, but there were no signs that a woman lived there, and I realized that Caspar had lied to me. I walked home, pushing my bicycle before me, stopping twice to sit by the side of the road until I was able to continue.

Felix left immediately for Berlin upon hearing the news and returned three days later in despair. He'd discovered nothing, except that many of his old friends were no longer willing or able to help him. Dorothea remained in her room for several days.

It took me a week to make a list of camps, people not wanting to talk about them, or even to admit that they existed. My plan was to send letters to Herr Elias at two different camps each month—Budzyn, Auschwitz, Gross-Rosen, Soldau, Sachsenhausen, Flossenbürg, Minsk, Riga, Westerbork, Dachau, Ravensbrück, Zimony, Sobibor, Theresienstadt (where privileged Jews and former members of the military were kept), Fuhlsbüttel, Treblinka, and Chelmno. When I reached the end of the list, I would start again.

Caspar found the body of Herr Elias's ginger cat in the woods, its fur stripped from its back and tail. When Dorothea at last left her room, I returned her embroidered handkerchief to her. She looked at me for a moment, then turned away, her hand over her mouth.

1943

The butcher in the village disappeared that winter with his wife and twin sons, and yet I was sure that I saw him at the mill in March. An object left momentarily on a table—an inkwell or a branch of witch hazel carried from the woods—was gone when I returned for it, and an apple or a dish of almonds disappeared even if I hadn't left the room.

One night a month after Herr Elias's disappearance, I thought that I could hear thunder, but I decided that it was only the hundreds of military transports on their way to the Eastern Front. When the rumbling sound grew louder and the earth began to shake, I knew that it wasn't the lorries but the hum of hundreds of planes.

A piercing, high-pitched sound like a scream grew louder and louder, and there was the flash and bellow of an explosion. The Yellow Palace shuddered violently twice, and across the park, smoke began to rise from the Pavilion. The oaks marking the path to the stables burst into flames. The temple with the striped awning had disappeared. I thought how strange it was that only moments before I'd been listening in the dark to the applause of a concert audience as *The Magic Flute* came to an end.

Dorothea lay facedown in the stable yard, her hands over her head as the dogs swarmed over her back and legs, barking and nipping in excitement. I grabbed her hand and pulled her to her feet. We ran across the yard to the root cellar that Caspar had made into a bomb shelter, the dogs chasing us in frenzied dashes.

It was dark in the root cellar, despite the lantern in Kreck's hand. The air was thick with the smell of loam (the smell of the grave, Kreck shouted). He sat with Roeder on one of the benches of cracked green leather that Caspar had taken from the baroness's carriages. Dorothea found a place between them, sitting in silence as she stared at her bare feet. I realized from her expression that she'd lost her hearing in the explosion. Caspar was not there. Felix gave Dorothea his jacket and stood on the stairs, where he watched the Yellow Palace burn to the ground. I whispered to myself the Evening Prayer I'd learned as a child. *Lighten our darkness, O Lord, we pray and in your great mercy defend us from all perils and dangers of this night, for the love of your only Son.* After two hours, the last of the planes, undisturbed by German fighters, swung north for the short trip to Berlin, and Dorothea, her hearing restored, rose like a tram passenger whose stop had at last arrived.

Across the park, smoke rose in billows. The statues bought by the Schumachers on their honeymoon in Naples lay across the terrace in a tumble of arms and heads. The Yellow Palace was in ashes. All of the ravishing objects that Felix had been unable to live without and the many objects essential to everyday life were gone. The garage and the stables had not been bombed, but it was still too hot for us to approach the Yellow Palace, and we walked across the park to the Pavilion.

Although there was smoke in some of the rooms, only the nursery and the conservatory were damaged. In the pantry, dozens of jars of preserves had exploded, and Dorothea said that we could lick the walls when we were hungry. We sat in the kitchen instead and drank two bottles of Mondeuse Blanche and ate the smoked oysters that Roeder had been saving for her nephew's wedding (she'd kept the tins in the Pavilion so that she wouldn't be tempted to eat them). We talked in loud voices, gesturing wildly, perhaps because of the wine, but more likely because we were alive.

It was light when we finally went to bed. Roeder, Schmidt, and I took three rooms on the second floor. Dorothea and Felix were in her parents' old bedrooms. Kreck and Caspar slept on field cots in the hall, the better to keep watch. *Cranes divide the night into sentry-duty and they make up the sequence of the watches by order of rank, holding little stones in their claws to ward off sleep. When there is danger they make a loud cry.*

.　　　.　　　.

Two of the Albanian workers who'd been assigned to labor in the village came to the Pavilion the following afternoon. The men had been sappers in the Resistance, and they offered to defuse an unexploded bomb lodged at the foot of a mulberry tree. Earlier in the year, Felix had noticed that the Albanians looked ill and hungry, and he'd arranged for them to take their meals at the village inn at his expense. The men were devoted to him.

After hours of combing the ruins with a garden rake, Roeder found a jewelry case with the bracelet and earrings that Felix had given Dorothea on their tenth wedding anniversary. Felix found a trunk with more jewels embedded in the lining, some melted gold coins, and several first editions—Ernest Hemingway and the *Fables* of La Fontaine—as well as a rolled-up Picasso that a friend had asked Felix to hide and that Felix had forgotten. I found a small metal casket with an ivory chess set and a drawing in brown ink of a nude woman and a peacock. That first day we found earthenware kegs of *Kirschwasser*, four large iron kettles, the concentric rings of the Schinkel chandelier, andirons, boot scrapers, a zinc bathtub, a steel trunk containing the baroness's Christmas ornaments, the metal spines of shoe trees, two large cured hams (they smelled delicious), and ceramic jars of pickled herring. When I showed Dorothea the drawing I'd found, she looked at it for a moment and said, "My father gave it to me for my seventeenth birthday. You must have it now." Before I could refuse, she turned to help Caspar drag pieces of a shattered urn onto the scorched lawn.

Later, we sat with the Albanians in the stables and ate ham and warm herring and drank more of Felix's wine as we listened to the wireless. Caspar, who'd taken shelter in the icehouse during the bombing, after returning to the stables for his radio, could find only German stations, each of them broadcasting a concert by Heinrich Schlusnus singing Schubert's "An Sylvia." Caspar, whose ferret had died of shock, said that the bombers that destroyed the Yellow Palace had been looking for the Daimler factory thirty miles west of Löwendorf, which they'd missed, perhaps because it was draped in netting sewn with half a million brown canvas rocks. In order to confuse the bombers further, clusters of red and green glowing balloons, called Christmas trees by the local people, were released nightly over the countryside, and many villages had been destroyed. The ruby and emerald stars that I saw in the sky over the Yellow Palace had led the bombers to Löwendorf.

As all of our belongings had been lost, we were allowed to choose articles of clothing from the trunks stored in the cellar of the Pavilion (we looked through them as carefully as if we were shopping at Wertheim's). As we sorted through the trunks, selecting things for ourselves and laying them aside, already covetous and possessive, Kreck pointed to his black monocle and whispered that Hitler had ordered the call-up of all German men between the ages of sixteen and sixty, regardless of illness or injury. When I said that Felix would never allow them to take him or Caspar, he gave me a weary smile.

I chose three summer cardigans, tweed trousers, three skirts, a pair of boots, a Victorian nightgown, wool ski socks, Felix's tennis flannels, and a necktie to use as a belt. Kreck dressed himself in a linen suit jacket and dress shirt, the arms too long, with tweed plus fours and gaiters. Roeder, wearing one of Felix's gray school blazers and a paisley shawl for a skirt, looked the oddest of all, perhaps because we were accustomed to her long black dress.

Two young women from the village who once worked in the Yellow Palace as laundresses, Frau Hoffeldt and Frau Bodenschatz, arrived at the Pavilion with their two girls and three boys, carrying what little bedding and clothing they'd managed to save from their houses. Their husbands had been taken prisoner at Kharkov that winter, and the bombing had left them without shelter or food. Twelve people in the village had been killed, and houses and farms destroyed. The women and their children moved into empty rooms above the stables, next to Caspar, where they were joined later in the week by a group of five foreign women, one of whom was pregnant, six children of different ages, and three men, who claimed to have walked from Odessa, eight hundred miles away. The weary but surprisingly healthy women told Felix, who spoke Russian, that it had taken them four months to reach Berlin, sleeping in abandoned houses by day and traveling at night. They'd bartered what little they had for milk and vegetables, and when they had no more to trade, they had, they were ashamed to say, resorted to theft. The men were escaped French slave workers, who'd fallen in with the women near Budapest, and to whom the women were indebted. There were many times, the women said, when the Frenchmen had to pretend that they were their husbands, and they had never abused their roles. When one of the women, Madame Tkvarcheli, released the hand of her pretty sixteen-year-old daughter, Bresla, having held it, according to one of the Frenchman, for the entire journey, there was soft applause.

The Russian Orthodox Easter was celebrated at the end of April, and Madame Tkvarcheli and the women insisted on making us a feast in the stables. We had roast squirrel, homemade vodka, mint tea, and black-currant jam. The children painted ducks' eggs with Dorothea's French watercolors (to their disappointment, we immediately ate the eggs). One of the women had a mouth organ and the children danced to a folk song called "Kalinka." Felix explained that the song compares the beloved to a snowberry, a raspberry, and a pine tree, which I thought was very apt.

In November, Felix asked if I would accompany Dorothea to Berlin, as she needed to see her doctor, Herr Professor Müller, whose clinic was in the north of the city. She'd not been able to reach him on the telephone, and she required his care. As Dieter had been hoarding petrol for just such an emergency, he would drive us to Professor Müller's clinic and wait for us before driving back to Löwendorf.

I hadn't been to the city since my afternoon with Felix at the Adlon, and I dreaded the trip. It wasn't the bombing that I feared (there'd been only nine raids in Berlin that year), but the SS and the Gestapo. Sensing my reluctance—as if I had the choice of remaining behind—he apologized that he was unable to go with us, as he had important business in Ludwigsfelde. Although I was frightened, I told him that I would be happy to accompany Dorothea to Berlin. Foreigners and even Germans who looked prosperous were often attacked (we would be riding in the Rolls-Royce, driven by a chauffeur in livery), and Caspar wanted me to carry his revolver, which I refused. Dorothea dressed me in some of her clothes, salvaged from trunks in the Pavilion—a brown Chanel coat, organdy skirt, Nordic ski sweater, and a pair of leather boots (they fit perfectly)—and we left for Berlin.

At first, the countryside seemed deceptively the same, although loose cattle and horses plunged back and forth across the roads, forcing Dieter (dressed, to my relief, in a sweater and trousers) to swerve out of their path. As we passed the Potsdam lake, beams of light were reflected from what looked like a row of submerged crucifixes. Dieter explained that the metal crosses had been placed just beneath the surface of the water to bounce back the radar signals of the Allied bombers. In October, the RAF had dropped hundreds of flares over Hannover, tricking German defenses, and then, without releasing a single bomb, had flown to Kassel, where they then dropped everything they had—a wicked ploy that could never happen in Potsdam, thanks to the crosses in the lake.

As we reached Schöneberg, a young man running alongside the car said there'd been an air raid in Berlin the previous night. A long convoy of lorries on its way to the Eastern Front moved slowly toward us, horns blaring to scatter the growing number of frightened people in the road, and Dieter had to pull into a field until it passed. It was thanks only to his persistence, which at times seemed deranged, that we were able to enter the city.

We were still some distance from Professor Müller's clinic when Dorothea told Dieter to take us instead to the gallery of her friend Hans Kreutzer. It was already late afternoon. If the bombers returned—they arrived promptly at seven o'clock, Dieter said—we would spend the night at the small flat she kept in Goethestrasse. If the flat had been bombed, Dieter would take us to her father's villa in Dahlem. If that, too, had been bombed, we'd have no choice but to return to Löwendorf.

Men and women climbed over the smoking piles of brick and rubble. Children sat in the ruins, their faces burned black. Streams of refugees wandered past, then wandered back again. Even though the windows were closed, there was a sharp smell of burning rubber and petrol. I heard sirens, but there were no fire engines or ambulances. When I asked Dorothea if we shouldn't return immediately to Löwendorf, she didn't answer. When I asked again, she shook her head, turning to stare into the street.

I knew that Herr Kreutzer sold books, many of them by writers banned by the party, as well as the occasional illuminated manuscript or painting taken as a favor on consignment. Herr Kreutzer sometimes even gave exhibitions. In a show of classical sculpture at the start of the war, a statue of a slender nude boy had been removed by the Gestapo, who found it suggestive of hunger, while a sculpture of a woman with large breasts and thighs had been permitted to remain as an example of contented maternity. Every few months, Herr Kreutzer packed his books and pictures, assisted by a young Polish prisoner of war he'd found hiding in his shop, and moved to a new address.

The gallery was in one of two buildings left standing on Hardenbergstrasse. Dorothea recognized it as the former salon of her couturière, who had disappeared that summer. The rooms were littered with bricks, wet bolts of cloth, and broken champagne bottles. Dressmaker forms lay across the floor like headless, armless torsos, the names barely visible— KRONPRINZESSIN CECILIE, FRÄULEIN KITTY, MLLE. LIDA BAAROVA. Herr Kreutzer's books and gramophone records were in cardboard boxes on four rickety gilt tables. He was not there, but a young man, presumably the Pole, sat on a mound of bricks, a notebook and pencil in his hand.

"Yes?" he asked coolly as we stepped around a shattered mirror.

Dorothea said that we were there to buy books, which she wished to be sent to friends in prison. "To everyone's continued amazement," she said, "including the Nazis themselves, the Gestapo still allows prisoners to receive parcels and letters." She looked through the boxes, making two piles of books, and gave the young man the names of twelve people and the prisons where the books were to be sent. When she finished, I asked if we could send some books to Herr Elias.

"But we don't know where they've taken him," she said quietly. At my expression, she said, "Yes, please do find some books for him."

I chose a collection of short stories by Thomas Mann, a biography of Duke Ellington, and a novel by Joseph Roth as the man repeated the names and addresses to Dorothea. She corrected one or two spellings (paying with an emerald brooch), and we left the shop, taking Herr Elias's books with us. As we stepped into the street, there was a loud undulating wail—I'd never heard anything like it, and I was frightened. Dieter had disappeared, but we weren't far from the Zoo Station, and we joined the crowd hurrying there.

Inside the flak tower, we stood with ten thousand people in two cavernous rooms. I could feel Dorothea trembling beside me, and I remembered that she was fearful in crowds ("Claustrophobia has me by the *neck*," she once whispered in a rural train station in which there were two other people). The crowd, groaning and swaying around us, emitted a smell of camphor, old sweat, and wet wool. A young woman standing next to me suddenly disappeared—as it was impossible to fall in any direction, she had simply folded into herself and sunk to the floor. In the effort first to find her and then to lift her, I lost Herr Elias's books.

The flat monotone of a woman's voice on the loudspeaker made it difficult to talk: "Five hundred B-17 and two hundred B-24 bombers are now overhead, accompanied by five hundred seventy-five fighters of the Royal Air Force. Seventeen British bombers in the first wave have been shot down, and several parachutists have been spotted over the southern suburbs." I added the numbers quickly—more than twelve hundred planes! I felt very proud, forgetting for a moment that the planes were dropping their bombs on *me*. I wondered if Mr. Knox's cousin was in one of the squadrons. The irony, as Felix might have said, was compelling.

Although we were in near darkness, Dorothea was sure that she saw Princess Dadiani, the companion of the French ambassador Monsieur Scapini. Dorothea called out to her, but her voice could not be heard over the loudspeaker and the moaning of the crowd. She shouted in my ear that Scapini had once told her that Africa would be extremely useful in any negotiations after the war, as Africa belonged to Europe.

We were released after two hours, but it took another hour to get out of the tower, directed by coldly inefficient twelve-year-old girls from the Bund Deutscher Mädel. In the street, the thick smoke made it difficult to see. We pushed our way through the crowd, our eyes burning. Broken glass splintered under our feet like ice. Ragtag groups of the Home Guard appeared suddenly out of the smoke, then ran away. When we at last reached Goethestrasse, we saw to our relief that the building where Dorothea had a flat was unharmed.

Her rooms were on the ground floor of a former royal villa that had been a gift from the last emperor to his favorite mistress. A garden ran along one side of the house, with four Japanese maples, their bark bright pink in the fading light. There was a kitchen and a bathroom, and a sitting room that also served as the bedroom, with French doors leading to the garden. The walls were bare. On either side of the fireplace were pale squares where there'd once been portraits of two royal jesters by Velázquez. "They're in the bank," she said when she saw me looking at the wall.

There was no heat or electricity, no lamp oil or firewood. I found two candelabra and lit the candles. We were filthy with soot and ash, but there was no water, and we were too cold to undress. She pushed the books and papers from a large bed onto the floor and lay down in her coat, placing one arm over her eyes. I was uncertain what to do.

"Come lie down," she called from the bed. "Felix prefers it here at night." She uncovered her eyes. "In candlelight. Just like this."

I found myself wondering if a life devoted to achieving perfection might not be somewhat trying. I'd learned to distinguish one thing from another (I knew that her chairs were Louis Seize), but the compulsion to limit the world to the exquisite seemed an increasingly meaningless affectation (as opposed to my affectation of courage). The water lilies rushed from the Buckow lake half an hour before the arrival of guests and placed among porcelain water lilies so that no one could tell the difference, the table set with Catherine the Great's swan dinner service, Felix's amber birdcages filled with live lovebirds and Xing dynasty enamel parrots (I'd described the lovebirds in one of my letters to Mr. Knox, but he had never referred to them and I realized belatedly that birds caged for effect would not have appealed to him).

"That world no longer exists," Dorothea said as if she could read my mind. "Its disappearance is of less significance than you like to think. Even beauty is of less importance now. Besides, Felix was always more interested in intelligence and wit. And style, of course." She smiled. "Although anyone extremely rich was allowed to be stupid."

I looked at the chairs, wondering if they were witty.

"It was difficult at first," she said, raising herself to lean against the pillows. "I was eighteen when we married. Four years younger than you are now. He had never been married, had no children, had grown up indulged and adored with only a younger sister to torment. His father had died in the Great War, and he lived in Paris with his mother and her lover.

"I was sent to live with my grandfather in London after my father exiled my mother to Löwendorf. My great-grandfather had been banker to Queen Victoria, and she had appointed him honorary consul in gratitude. I first met Felix at one of my grandfather's dinner parties. He came with his mistress, an older American woman who was a photographer. It was the first time I'd seen a woman other than an army nurse in khaki. They'd come from Nepal, where the American had been taking pictures of snow leopards. I fell in love with Felix that night, as did several other women in the room. He was taking the photographer the next day to see the Isenheim Altarpiece in Colmar. They were staying near Baden in a monastery where the monks wear white cassocks and black opera hats. No one seemed to think these things exceptional—white leopards, American mistresses in khaki, monks in silk opera hats—and I learned to accept such things as commonplace." She rested her head on the pillows.

As I watched her, I realized that I, too, had come to view certain things as commonplace—adulterous countesses, impotent Egyptian princes, movie stars in ermine stoles. Nothing as exotic as white leopards, perhaps, but once shocking to a girl from Ballycarra.

She lit a cigarette with one of the candles. "I convinced my perfectly healthy grandfather that he was in need of taking the waters, and three days later, we happened to meet Felix and his friend sitting before Grünewald's green Christ. I was furious that he took no notice of me and I announced that I wasn't at all sure that I liked the altarpiece, one of the most beautiful things in the world. A trick that I would have thought rather obvious, but it worked. He suggested that I read Rousseau, who despised Gothic art—it would help to sharpen my desires. Despite my obvious fascination, he treated me like the child that I was, aside from the reference to desires in need of sharpening (something which, I might add, he never mentioned again). It was only when we saw each other a year later in Paris, a meeting I also contrived, that he spoke to me as if no one else were present, although only to ask if I was familiar with the memoirs of Saint-Simon. I was fifteen years old, and I knew that if he did not love me, I would die." She paused. "Fortunately, my inclination to indolence kept me from further rashness. Although I did read Saint-Simon."

"And here you are."

"Yes," she said, looking around the room. "Here I am."

"And you didn't die."

"Whether Felix loves me or not remains a mystery. A mystery I hope never to solve."

I sat in one of the chairs. I'd never known Dorothea to be melodramatic, and it disappointed me. It was the most she had said to me in five years, and she wasn't finished.

"His life was a torment of interests—an excursion to Mesopotamia to look for artifacts was as intensely experienced as the season's new melons. He had ideas about everything. How something should look or taste or smell. How a person should behave. For someone who mistrusted opinions, he had more rules than anyone I'd ever known. He would have said that these views were only his own, but I had to learn his rules very fast. I disappointed him our first night together by wearing a blue dressing gown in a gray-and-red bedroom."

"What color should you have worn?"

"Black. Red."

I was silent, thinking about the shades of color suitable for a dressing gown in a gray-and-red bedroom. Felix's exaggerated manner, no matter how refined—perhaps because of its refinement—would have seemed artificial and even forced had it not been for Dorothea. She was no less refined, no less complicit than Felix. She just wasn't adamant about it.

"I discovered to my surprise that taste can be very inconsistent. Someone may be impeccable about food, but not dress well. Someone's rooms might be charming, but you dread dining at home with him, and know not to ask what he is reading. But Felix was really rather perfect. His great flaw—his sister liked to say it was his only flaw—was his endless capacity for boredom. I could recognize the moment, and unfortunately it came rather soon, when he began to lose interest—there was a change in the color of his eyes. That is when I would remind him that boredom is really one of the least terrible things in the world." She paused. "I speak of him in the past tense because he has changed."

I wondered if he was ever bored with me. I wouldn't have been able to bear it if he was tired of me. "Why have you kept me?" I asked.

"Felix says that you are ready to steal horses with us." At my look of surprise, she said, "It's a German expression. It's not that we've kept you. You've kept us. We sometimes wonder why. You're an Irish citizen. There's nothing to stop you from leaving."

"It's too late."

"At the start of the war, when Felix refused the posting in Madrid, people said that he was frivolous. He would once again be in a position of power and, most important of all, we would be out of the country. Even our friends were mystified."

"People think he's a spy."

Her face, naturally very pale, was gray with strain. "The truth is that Ribbentrop told Felix that he would have to divorce me if he accepted a post." There was the sudden moan of sirens, and she jumped from the bed. "What would Felix have us do?" she asked, her voice rising. "The most *he* does is ask Kreck to close the shutters. It is a relief that they've come. It will only last an hour. They won't come twice. Surely."

She'd heard that there was a private air-raid shelter at the Spanish embassy across the square, and we decided to go there. We quickly put on our hats, and I blew out the candles. There were few people in the street, and I wondered if perhaps we'd left it a bit late. There was a loud droning hum that could only signal the approach of hundreds of planes. My mouth was dry, and my eyes burned. She took hold of my sleeve and found my hand. "Are you afraid?" she asked. "I am a bit. The only dangerous animal to have escaped from the zoo was a terrified gray wolf, not a tiger, and he was found last week hiding in a bush behind the Opera, extremely relieved to be captured."

We crossed the square and ran up the steps of the embassy. The heavy front gate was unlocked, and we pushed our way inside, stumbling over furniture as we ran through a number of large rooms. I was sure that I touched something alive in the third room, perhaps a cat, and I lit the candle I'd put in my pocket when we left the flat.

To our surprise, sitting on a sofa in front of us was an elderly man in a wool dressing gown and carpet slippers. He berated us for disturbing him but stopped when he recognized Dorothea. It was the ambassador. "Fool!" he shouted at me. "Put out that candle."

The droning sound had increased to a roar, and the walls began to shake. There was the piercing whine of falling bombs. I blew out the candle, and we threw ourselves onto the sofa, my head wedged beneath Dorothea's arm, our legs entwined. The ambassador, smelling of brandy and singed wool, seemed to be breathing with difficulty, perhaps because we were on top of him, and we moved so as not to suffocate him. I'd wet myself, and there was a smell of urine—for a moment I dreaded the smell more than I did the bombs.

As the first wave of bombers passed overhead, a second wave could be heard approaching. The raid lasted for more than an hour, the nearby flak tower at Zoo firing its antiaircraft guns without cease. The tower was several streets away, but it sounded as if the guns were on the roof of the embassy. When it was at last silent, the ambassador kicked us in the ribs, knocking us to the floor.

I was shaking with cold, thanks in part to my wet skirt and stockings, and I struggled to my feet to light the candle as Dorothea searched for our hats. Gathering his dressing gown around his bare legs, the ambassador reached under the sofa for a bottle and took a long drink. Holding the brandy tightly by the neck, he said that as he hadn't expected us, he had no glasses. No food, either, he added quickly. "And there's no private shelter. It's a canard started by that pig, the Japanese ambassador." He struggled irritably to his feet to kiss Dorothea's hand. We said good night and found our way to the street.

It seemed as if all of Berlin was burning. Some buildings were still standing, while alongside them others had vanished. Burned cars and lorries lay twisted in the street. A lone Hitler Youth stood on a corner, screaming over and over again that the Charlottenburg Palace was on fire. The row of embassies on the north side of the square had disappeared, and a dense cloud of dust had settled in the few trees that remained. We could hear the cries of people trapped in buildings. Old men and women and children, pale with ash, emerged from shelters as if walking in their sleep. Figures stood in silhouette before the burning buildings, looking like devils in a morality play. There was a danger, I knew, of the concussion of air that occurs after a bombing, and I walked with my hands over my mouth, as if that would save me.

It took us several hours to cross the square, stopping every few steps to help the injured and the dying, and it was near daybreak when we at last crept into the flat, ashamed that it was unharmed, ashamed that we were unharmed, but grateful, too. We stood in the center of the room, shaking with cold. Dorothea found blankets, three jars of potted shrimp, and two bottles of champagne. We sat in silence on the bed, the blankets around our shoulders, and ate the shrimp and drank champagne, our hands marked with dried blood. When we'd eaten all of the shrimp, we crawled under the blankets. Dorothea fell into a heavy sleep, but I lay there until dawn, convinced that I'd lost something of great importance, something that would cause our deaths if I did not find it, when I at last fell asleep.

We awoke in the early afternoon, drank the second bottle of champagne, and went into the street. Children, many of them burned, wandered through the smoke and dust, and injured men and women lay by the side of the road. There was no color except for the red of the fires.

It was a sign of our shock that we felt no surprise to find Dieter waiting at the end of the street. He'd spent the night in a shelter, afraid that he would not make it to Berlin if he returned to Löwendorf. Seeing that we were safe, he allowed himself a burst of temper. "It's a miracle you're alive," he shouted in fury. "And the villa still standing!"

"I'll never see it again," Dorothea said quietly to me.

The windows of the car had been shattered, but the motor turned over when he started it, and we climbed into the backseat. We stopped to pick up a family with four children, taking them as far as the road to Zurich. Dorothea gave them what money she had, and her own as well as my coat and gloves. Afraid that she would give them the boots, I sat with my legs hidden beneath me, but it was of no use. The woman left wearing Dorothea's lovely boots.

That night, at last safe in my bed in the Pavilion—the American bombers passed overhead for two hours on their way to Berlin—I wondered where I would go if I were to leave Löwendorf. I didn't have relatives in Zurich who would help me, even if I could make my way five hundred miles to the border. When I left Ireland, I'd felt, for all the recklessness of my flight, that I'd at last pushed off—I'd been set in motion, and I would find the world I so greedily sought, but I saw that night that the world had found me.

1944

F elix's cousin, Herr Prazan, and his wife arrived one morning
from Joslitz, their estate south of Prague. Although Joslitz
had been requisitioned for the use of an SS commandant, the
Prazans had continued to live in the house, confined to the
south wing. Felix was not at home. Dorothea explained that
while she had little to offer—we were living on small rations of
potatoes, carrots, wild garlic, jam, and schnapps (which left us
in a state of mild drunkenness)—they were welcome to stay for
lunch, which was our one meal of the day.

In the dining room, Herr Prazan told Dorothea that life in
Prague had been easy in comparison with the lives of relatives

in Hamburg, where forty-five thousand people had been killed in a single night's bombing. "Our Czech friends, as no doubt you are aware, don't like the Gestapo very much, and they certainly didn't take to Reichsprotektor Heydrich, but at least they cannot be conscripted, and there are still marvelous opportunities to turn a profit. The Czechs have one goal only, and that is survival. They may despise their masters, but they are quite happy to serve them."

I saw that with each pronouncement, Dorothea grew more and more agitated, until she at last interrupted Prazan to say that Reichsprotektor Heydrich had participated in devising the Reich's plan of extermination, which had already resulted in the deaths of hundreds of thousands of innocent people. Prazan raised his eyebrows as if Dorothea were a difficult child, and said that if she was referring to the rumors of extermination camps, those stories were unjust and unproved. Surely she didn't believe them. He was leaving Joslitz only because he expected the Russians, whose arrival was inevitable, would make German landowners like himself pay for Stalingrad, among other unfortunate mishaps, and that despite her deplorable sympathies, the Russians would not spare Löwendorf, either. "Although," he said with a malicious smile, looking around the empty dining room, "this isn't the Yellow Palace."

Dorothea rang the bell for Kreck to clear the table, even though we hadn't finished our soup. She told the Prazans that a number of refugees had arrived that morning, some of them Czech, whose will to survive had fortunately brought them as far as Löwendorf. As she had much work to do before nightfall, she would have to bid the Prazans good-bye. She hoped never to see them again.

Herr Prazan, slowly wiping his mouth, said that he'd been warned that his *chère cousine* was sympathetic to the Reds and had for some years heard rumors about her own family too scandalous to repeat. He, for one, had never allowed himself to believe them, but he now saw that he'd been mistaken. As he spoke, Frau Prazan silently drained her glass of schnapps and then reached across the table for Dorothea's glass and emptied that, too. She slid her hand in my direction, but I picked up my glass just in time. Herr Prazan took his wife's arm, and they left the room, finding their own way to the door.

Later when we went to the stable yard, the Czech refugees, looking momentarily dazed, having already finished what remained of our lunch, asked when they might expect supper.

Kreck told me that Frau Prazan had taken three gray linen napkins with her when she left. The ones that had so delighted me when I first arrived at Löwendorf with their silhouette of Zara, the donkey.

By the end of February, I'd sent forty-four letters to Herr Elias. As I learned the names of more camps, I added them to the list—Stargard, Woldenberg, Luckenwalde, Alt-Drewitz, Oschatz, Natzweiler-Struthof, Neuengamme, Dora, Potulice, Bergen-Belsen, Jaworzno, Zgoda, and Colditz Castle.

Because the bombers passed overhead every few nights, a wheezing trumpet, blown by Caspar, sounded promptly each night at six fifteen to announce the approach of the planes, whether they had been sighted or not. There were sometimes five hundred RAF planes in the sky, escorted by one hundred Mosquito fighters.

We pulled on as many of our borrowed clothes as we could manage, lest we have to join the refugees on the road, and waddled across the lawn to the root cellar, already jammed with people—Frau Hoffeldt and Frau Bodenschatz and their five children, Madame Tkvarcheli, her daughter, Bresla, and the three other Black Sea women and their children, as well as the Frenchmen. The crowded cellar reminded me of pictures I'd seen of emigrants in the hold of a ship.

The Frenchmen, whose names were Lazare, Bertrand, and Maxime, chattered incessantly, perhaps from nerves, and when Dorothea was not too agitated, she translated for them. They claimed that the best slave workers in the world were Russian (with a gentlemanly nod to the Odessa women and, in particular, to Bresla), and the worst were the Italians. They had dreaded working alongside an Italian, who whined bitterly while he devised ingenious ways to avoid his share of the work. All of the Russian workers had been young unmarried women, which also may have been why the Frenchmen preferred them to Italians.

Bored with their own stories of life in occupied Budapest, the men had the idea to recite the lines of their favorite movie, *La Kermesse Héroique*. They performed only a little of the story each night, Felix and Dorothea translating into Russian and German, and we soon found ourselves longing for the sound of the trumpet (Kreck said that Lazare's miming of a Spaniard using a fork for the first time was the best thing he'd ever seen). Would the duke allow the mayor's daughter to marry the painter? Would the shrewd Cornelia save the town from the wicked Spanish? I could see why the Nazis had banned the film (unlike Laurel and Hardy and *Tarzan of the Apes*). On those nights when it was impossible to hear the Frenchmen, we sat in glum silence—even the dogs were disappointed. When the planes at last passed overhead, we emerged to a black sky full of stars, stricken with a sudden and exhilarating happiness.

For the first time in years, Dorothea, perhaps inspired by the Frenchmen, wished to celebrate Christmas. The Odessa women made a *tableau vivant* of the Nativity, using Zara (miraculously alive, like Count von Arnstadt, although for different reasons—no one wanted to eat the count yet), the children, and the always-obliging Frenchmen—one beast of burden, five blond angels, and three shepherds in berets. Kreck was put to use as one of the Magi. Bresla was a chaste Mary, eyes lowered and hands clasped at her breast. Felix made a dignified St. Joseph, draped in a striped beach towel from Hermès. The Christ Child was a real baby, born that October to Bresla's aunt ("Yet another Immaculate Conception," whispered Kreck). Caspar and I were angels, wearing sheets, and wings made of cardboard and a few feathers. We drank the last of the *Kirschwasser* saved from the Yellow Palace and ate turnips roasted with wild garlic, and dried pears. Caspar had spread boughs of juniper across the floor, and the stables were as fragrant as a forest. There was music and an attempt at dancing, but despite the *Kirschwasser* and the charm of the children, our spirits were very low.

Caspar gave me a small pin box made from his collection of fossils. Felix gave me two of his own books—*Die Marquise von O* and *The Glass Key*. I made handkerchiefs for everyone, the women's crocheted with string. Very useful in time of war, said Felix (I wasn't sure if he was teasing me—he might have meant it).

The day after Christmas, Frau Schmidt asked Dorothea's permission to return to her family in Ludwigsfelde. She'd worked for the Metzenburgs for thirty years, but she wished, she said, to die at home. And, she added as an afterthought, displaying humor that I hadn't known she possessed, there was nothing left to cook. Dorothea gave her some potatoes and a bundle of warm clothes to take with her. I thought that there would be tears, but Frau Schmidt couldn't wait to be gone.

Caspar and I were stunned to hear on the wireless that the Americans had landed in France. We ran to find Dorothea and Felix, who were listening to the news with Kreck and Roeder. On Berlin radio, which was the only frequency that Felix could find, there were descriptions of thousands of American dead in a failed Allied attempt to invade France—the coast of Normandy, said the German announcer, was red with the blood of the defeated enemy.

Rumors of the landing quickly spread, and the women and the Frenchmen joined us in the library, sitting on the floor, the children in their laps. Almost two hours after the first report, Caspar, who manipulated the dials at Felix's request, at last found a special BBC news bulletin, broadcast in English and German. "In the early hours of Sunday, the sixth of June, bombers of the Royal Air Force dropped aluminum foil over Calais in the hope of deceiving the radar into believing that an invasion was under way. Meanwhile, more than seven thousand vessels, the largest naval task force ever assembled, moved under darkness to the Normandy coast. Shortly after midnight, the British 6th and American 101st and 82nd Airborne Divisions began their landing. The Americans landed under heavy cloud cover and extensive enemy flak, causing them to be dropped over an area of one thousand square miles. This caused the Germans great confusion . . ."

The refugee women, who did not speak English or German, stared at the wireless as if in a trance. When the program was interrupted, Caspar jumped to his feet to mime the actions of the Allies—swimming, rifle held over his head, firing the rifle, and then crawling on his belly—much to the women's terror. As I watched him, I thought of the simplicity of the defenses used by both sides, some of which had once made me laugh—sunken metal crucifixes, nets sewn with canvas rocks, green and red Christmas lights, aluminum foil—and I felt ashamed.

In the morning, we gathered in Caspar's room to listen to Churchill's address to the House of Commons, broadcast on a Swiss station. "I cannot, of course, commit myself to any particular details. Reports are coming in rapid succession. So far the Commanders who are engaged report that everything is proceeding according to plan. And what a plan! This vast operation is undoubtedly the most complicated and difficult that has ever taken place. It involves tides, wind, waves, visibility, both from the air and the sea standpoint, and the combined employment of land, air, and sea forces in the highest degree of intimacy and in contact with conditions which could not and cannot be fully foreseen . . . Many dangers and difficulties which at this time last night appeared extremely formidable are behind us." The Allies had ten thousand dead, but losses were lighter than had been feared. The Germans were said to have half a million dead, which shocked us.

In the following days, the news that we heard on Swiss and English stations was so contradictory that it was impossible to know what to believe—we were exultant one moment and distraught the next. The previous summer, when the Germans had announced a turning point in the war that could only lead to victory thanks to the launching of V-1 and V-2 rockets against London, we'd learned not to trust the reports. For years we had observed the discrepancy between the German news and what we ourselves saw and heard, and we no longer trusted anything broadcast over German radio, including the music.

The Americans, who had chosen not to believe that Jews and other human beings objectionable to the Reich had been systematically murdered for years, were said, according to a Swiss broadcast, to have at last accepted the testimony of two escaped prisoners from Auschwitz, a Mr. Rudolf Vrba and a Mr. Alfred Wetzler, admitting as fact what we had known for some time.

. . .

On the twentieth of July, a program of Bruckner, conducted by Karajan in Berlin, was interrupted with a brief announcement that there had been an attempt to assassinate Hitler. There was no other news, and the station immediately went off the air, which made us wonder. Caspar tried to tell the Odessa women, but the verb "to attempt" was impossible to convey in gestures and, in his excitement, he mistakenly led them to believe that Hitler (mustache, goose step, Nazi salute) had been killed. The women fell to their knees to sing a hymn of thanks, and it took an hour for us to calm them, by which time all of us, including Caspar, were crying.

The assassination attempt on Hitler's life was not a rumor. Seven thousand people were arrested, half of whom were immediately hung without trial. Felix said that the plot was the belated and somewhat inefficient work of Count von Stauffenberg and his fellow officers in the Wehrmacht, including Count von Hartenfels, who had grown dissatisfied with the political and military goals of the Reich. Their discontent, Felix said, had nothing to do with the deportations and executions of Jews and dissidents or the civil policies of the Reich. The officers' aristocratic notions of honor had doomed the plot from the beginning. Not only was Hitler alive, but the hapless conspirators were dead. Count von Hartenfels and several officers, including Stauffenberg, had been executed by firing squad on the twenty-first of July in a courtyard lit by the headlights of a truck.

Count von Arnstadt told Felix that film of other executions—the conspirators hung by a wire suspended from a meat hook—was sent each night to the Führer for his private viewing. The first cameramen, disgusted by their assignment, had quit in protest, which quickly resulted in their own hanging. The count also told Felix that certain Germans in high positions had begun to approach their European and American counterparts to offer the release of certain prisoners (pilots, priests, scientists, and spies, among others) in exchange for foreign passports. Some arrangements had already been made. A set of false papers, which included a passport, travel permit, military pass, and Home Guard Z-pass, could also be bought for a bar of gold. "A yellow star," Arnstadt said, "costs three times as much, as it is thought that the Americans will be especially nice if they think you are a Jew."

The winter of 1944 was the coldest in a hundred years. The trees in the park bent in the wind like figures in flight, and the river was frozen from December until February. The last of the tundra swans disappeared, killed perhaps by the deserting soldiers moving in increasing numbers across the countryside, and Zara was stolen from the stables.

We heard reports of an uprising at the Birkenau camp in Poland. Those inmates who worked in the gas chambers had attacked their guards with stones and hammers, and although the guards quickly discovered the explosives smuggled into the camp by women inmates who worked in the nearby IG Farben factory, hundreds of prisoners managed to escape, only to be captured the next day. The women, who were tortured before their execution, refused to name the conspirators. I wondered, as I often did, if Herr Elias were still alive. I dreamed that he had escaped at Birkenau and eluded the guards, coming to us at Löwendorf.

Those nights when Caspar could not find a station on the wireless, we sat on his bed, huddled together for warmth, to discuss the day's rumors (I'd noticed that the farther you were from the front, the more accurate were the rumors). Sometimes there was even half a cup of acorn coffee to share, and we passed it back and forth in the dark, careful not to spill it, fingers touching.

A letter from Inéz was found in the fork of an elm by one of the children. Once again, she wrote to beg the Metzenburgs to flee Germany (the place that Churchill called the abode of the guilty). The army was abandoning its positions, and the Russians would soon be in Berlin. There were safe houses, she said, and people who would help them. When Dorothea read the letter to Felix, he said that he would never leave Germany, not after all that had happened. But that is exactly why we must leave, she said. He said that perhaps she should think about going without him.

I could see that she was offended that he could imagine living without her, of dying without her. For the first time in their married life, she was better able to cope than her husband, but if he was not able to leave Germany, she was not able to leave him. He offered to send Roeder and me away, but Roeder burst into tears at the thought of it. I told him that I, too, wished to remain at Löwendorf. We've come so far, I said. Dorothea quietly left the room.

One cold morning toward the end of the year, Roeder came to tell me that Felix, who had not been well, wished to see me. I went to him at once. He was in bed, *Anna Karenina* lying open on his chest. He seemed a bit feverish. His former look of indulgent tolerance had become simply a look of tolerance.

"There's no one else I can ask," he said. He reached under his pillow and pulled out a worn handkerchief to wipe the corners of his mouth. I began to speak, but he interrupted me. "In the cellar, hidden behind the coal chute, is a metal chest. Inside it, you will find a wooden panel. A painting."

I was to remove the panel, which would be wrapped in canvas, without looking at it, and take it to the village where men would be waiting for me in a car. I was to follow the car from the village. The men would take the painting from me. It was of the utmost importance that I not be seen with the men.

I did all that he said, except for one thing. It was a painting of a naked woman in a gold necklace and a hat trimmed in swans down. Her body was like Dorothea's body—small breasts, high waist, pale skin. Like Dorothea, she had a melancholy and foreboding beauty. She stood beneath an apple tree, one arm raised, as a stag and long-eared doe watched solemnly from the woods. At the foot of the tree, an unhappy cupid swatted the bees drawn to the honeycomb in his hand.

There were Latin verses in the upper right corner: *The pleasures of life are mixed with pain.*

I took my bike along the frozen river so as to avoid the road, stopping twice to tighten the string that bound the painting to the handlebars. It was difficult to see where I was going, and I jumped from the bike to push it along the icy path.

A black Daimler was parked in front of the inn. To my relief, the villagers ignored the car, perhaps because it was flying a small Nazi flag. A man in a Nazi uniform was driving, and a man wearing dark glasses sat in the backseat. I stood beneath the oak tree at the entrance to the village and checked my tires, shivering with cold. The driver threw his cigarette out the window and drove away. I counted to fifty and followed them. The car turned down an overgrown wagon track leading into the woods, and the driver parked in a grove of alder and stepped from the car.

Cutting the string with his pocket knife, he removed the painting from its wrapping. I saw that he held it with care, and I hoped that I hadn't damaged it. The man in the backseat opened his door and took the painting in his two hands. He didn't look at me, perhaps too entranced by what he saw. He said that he was sorry to hear that our friend was not well. *"Zu meiner Verwunderung hat er ein Mädchen geschickt."* I'm surprised that he sent a girl.

The driver handed me a bound copy of *Grimm's Fairy Tales*, inside of which was a brown envelope, and they drove away. I stood there, holding my bicycle. I hadn't said a word. I was too shaken to ride, and I walked the bicycle through the woods, the book under my arm. I went to Felix's room as soon as I reached the house. He seemed not to have moved since I left, *Anna Karenina* still open on his chest. I placed the book of fairy tales on a table next to the bed, and he closed his eyes.

I left a note for Kreck in the kitchen and went into the park. My shoes were soon soaked through, despite Kreck's assurance that they were waterproof (I'd traded him six pairs of socks for them). I began to run, not stopping until I reached the blackened earth where the little temple had once stood. Since the war began, I'd tried to be strong and courageous—not an unusual intention, given the people with whom I lived—but it had been harder than I'd imagined, and I wondered if I'd have the strength to continue.

The following day, Kreck found five large hampers in the stables. There were two hams, four cases of tinned sardines in tomato sauce, cartons of powdered milk, a large sack of Ethiopian coffee, four tins of English biscuits, wheels of cheese, two sides of bacon, a jar of mustard, two vats of sauerkraut, and a box of Swiss chocolates. Food was given to the refugees for dinner (they preferred to cook for themselves once Schmidt left), and what we didn't eat that night (very little as our stomachs were unsettled) was hidden in the cellar. "We'll live like kings," said Kreck, and for a while, we did.

1945

In March, news came that a thousand B-17 bombers of the United States Eighth Air Force had destroyed the center of Berlin in an attempt to stop the Sixth Panzer Army from reaching the Eastern Front. The bombing was so heavy that the fires, driven by high winds, burned for five days before the flames reached the canals and rivers that surround the city. The Reich Chancellery, Gestapo headquarters, and the despised People's Court were gone. Radio Paris, the station of Vichy France, reported that the raid would have resulted in even more death and destruction had it not been led by a Jewish lieutenant colonel named Rosenthal.

Swiss radio reported that soldiers of the advancing Red

Army had found eight thousand prisoners at the Birkenau camp, too weak and sick to join a forced march when their guards ordered the abandonment of the camp. Caspar thought that these reports helped to convince people that the war was coming to an end even more than the daily postings of dead, wounded, and captured German soldiers.

I had written more than seventy letters to Herr Elias, and I'd added more concentration camps to my list—Jungfernhof, Papenburg, Janowska, Donauwörth, Thorn, Hohnstein, Klooga, and Gradiška. They were everywhere.

The apple trees were in bud, and although many of the fruit trees had been cut for firewood, there would soon be apples and pears. I decided to walk to the Night Wood to see if the witch hazel was in bloom. The park was already in shadow when I left the yard, a faint mist moving through the trees. The junipers looked blue in the fading light. There'd been rain that afternoon, and the branches of the yews dragged on the wet ground. At the edge of the river, the reeds lay beaten against the bank.

As I hurried along, I saw a boy moving cautiously on the far side of the river—one of the young men who hid in the woods, stealing at night to his family's farm for supper and a warm bed before returning to the forest at dawn. A thrush jumped from tree to tree, as if to warn the boy of my approach, but he was from the village and knew that I meant him no harm. I waved to him. He lifted his cap and pointed to the wood.

It would be dark before I could reach the clearing at the center of the Night Wood, and I decided to walk only as far as the larch grove. As deer had not been seen at Löwendorf for several years, I was surprised to catch sight of one, bedding for the night in a stand of winterberry. I'd been reading the *Metamorphoses* and for a moment I thought that the deer was human—perhaps a bewitchment undone, an old spell reversed by a remorseful goddess. I stopped so as not to frighten it, but it was too late.

To my astonishment, it *was* a man. A torn shirt was knotted around his neck. His arms were covered with sores. His trousers were torn, and he was barefoot. A bloody rag was tied around his thigh.

I turned and ran, not stopping until I reached the park. My heart was beating in my throat, and I rested against the garden wall as I caught my breath, looking over my shoulder to make sure that he hadn't followed me. For a moment, I felt lightheaded.

Inside the house, a candle was lit and a shadow jumped along the walls of the passage. Smoke drifted from the chimney, and I wondered if Roeder, grown inventive in the kitchen, was making soup. I could hear the river. It would look black where it was deep, I knew, and silver in the shallows. I repeated a passage from one of Mr. Knox's books. *I am friend to the pilibeen, the red-necked chough, the parsnip land-rail . . . the common marsh-coot.*

He lay on his back on the path, his eyes closed. I poked him with the tip of my shoe, but he didn't move. Taking hold of his wrists, I dragged him slowly down the path, looking for a place to hide him. He was almost weightless, but I had lost my strength. I pulled him through an opening in the hedge that bordered the path and took hold of his ankles, easing him down a shallow bank into a dry streambed.

"American," he said in a hoarse whisper, startling me.

"If the Werewolves find you, they'll kill you. Perhaps they're watching us now." I sounded a bit wild, and I tried to calm myself.

"Werewolves?" he asked.

I found a candle stub and matches in my pocket and lit the candle, thinking again of Ovid, and of Psyche leaning over the sleeping Cupid. I realized from his expression that I was not in the least like Psyche, but an ugly witch, the candle flickering beneath my chin, and I blew out the candle (my vanity, even then!).

His eyes followed me as I crawled between the trees, collecting dead leaves and pine needles to tuck around his feet and pile on his chest. "Something I never did before, or even imagined," I heard him say. "A Pullman car! Me in a Pullman car, straight from my mother's house."

"I'll come for you tomorrow," I whispered, packing the leaves around his legs. He didn't seem to hear me. "There's a house nearby where you'll be safe," I said in a louder voice. I put my hand on his brow. He was burning with fever.

"There were leaks in the gas tanks," he said, brushing away my hand. "You had to keep your mask on even when you were sleeping, which I thought was pretty damn funny. How would you know you were dead if you were asleep? How would you know you were dead if you were dead? The point is you wouldn't." He made a harsh sound in his throat that I realized was a laugh.

"There were hundreds of gases, and we had to learn each one of them. Mustard gas smells like geraniums. Sarge said after the war is over I can use my natural instinct for smells to make good money. That's what he called it. My natural instinct for smells. Good money! Like there's bad money."

"I'll come for you tomorrow," I said again.

"What I'm really good at," he said, "is mortars. Almost as good as I am with gas. A mortar could clean every tree from this forest. I could clear out this whole goddamn forest." He glanced to either side, suddenly agitated. He curled one shoulder into his chest, wincing with pain as he tried to rise, and the leaves and pine needles I'd piled on his chest slid to the side. "My heart," he said. "It's loud in my throat."

Placing the matches and candle where he could reach them, I told him that I would bring someone in the morning, and we would carry him to a house where he'd be safe. He closed his eyes. His silence was a relief—I'd worried that he would talk through the night. I took off my coat and covered him with it.

Despite a yellow moon, the path was barely visible, and I twice took the wrong turning. My mind was racing even faster than my heart. There was no medicine at Löwendorf, no hospitals nearby, no doctors. Furze tea is good for scarlet fever, and monkshood in water, but I couldn't remember how many drops, and too much monkshood brings on a fatal freezing of the heart. Marsh pennywort grew by the river—a leaf applied to a cut stops bleeding—but there would be no leaves for months. Caspar would help me, but Kreck was too old and Felix too frail. There was Dorothea, but the two of us weren't strong enough to carry a wounded man as far as the Pavilion.

I suddenly wondered if he was real. My eyesight was cloudy, which is a symptom of starvation, and objects sometimes appeared blurred. For a moment, it was a relief to think that I'd imagined him.

As I turned into the stable yard, I saw the headlights of a car parked in front of the Pavilion. Felix was standing in the window of the drawing room, next to a man in a uniform and boots.

I went into the house. The officer had been at school with Felix in Heidelberg. He was on his way to Switzerland, where he would try to cross the border. I immediately thought of giving him my letters to Herr Elias to mail, and ran to find them. The officer, implicated in the plot against Hitler, had abandoned his command. He said that the roads were crowded with deserters and refugees. The Führer was refusing to admit defeat. Berlin was defended by twelve-year-old boys and old men.

The officer at last drove away with my letters and a bottle of schnapps. I began to tell Felix about the man in the Night Wood, but he stopped me to call Kreck into the room. He told Kreck to bring a bottle of champagne and to ask Roeder and Caspar to come to the drawing room. I went to the fire to warm myself. "Where have you been?" Dorothea asked with a frown. "And what have you done with your coat?"

Kreck returned with the champagne, followed by Roeder and Caspar, and I heard him whisper to Felix, "*Dies ist die letzte Flasche.*" This is the last bottle. He placed two glasses on a tray.

Felix made a rapid encircling gesture with his hand, and Kreck went to the sideboard, moving like a dog that has been trained to walk upright, where he poured six glasses of champagne, emptying the bottle. He gave a glass to Dorothea and to Felix, and then one to Caspar, Roeder, and myself. Kreck, with his turned-up Kaiser Wilhelm mustache, his eye singed from his head in service to the emperor, took, with a little soundless meeting of his slippered heels, the sixth glass for himself.

Later, I went to Dorothea's room to tell her about the American. Her room was cold, and I lit a fire. She was standing at the doors that led to the terrace, her arms folded tightly across her chest. She said that she'd learned that afternoon that her friend Sophia Plessen had been arrested and taken to Plötzensee prison, where she'd been executed. She said that she could no longer live in such a country. She no longer cared what Felix thought, or whether or not she left without him. Whether or not she died without him. She'd wanted to go ever since the disappearance of Herr Elias. I was welcome to go with her. She would never see Berlin again. The entire country disgusted her.

"There's a man in the woods," I said.

She began to pace. "There are hundreds of men in the woods," she said impatiently. "Thousands."

"An American."

She opened a dresser drawer, looked into it for several minutes, and closed it. She went to her writing desk, found her diary, and dropped it into a wastepaper basket. When she began to pull the blankets and sheets from her bed, I asked what she was doing.

"We'll want bedding, but nothing more." She attempted to fold an eiderdown into a square, then dropped it on the floor. "Won't you help?" she asked in irritation. When I didn't move, she said, "It's not even your country. What are you doing here?"

I led her to the bed. She lay on her side, suddenly quiet, and I covered her with the quilt. "Stay with me," she said. She began to hum, her hands over her ears. I climbed onto the bed and put my arm around her.

I was awakened by cries in the yard. Dorothea was not there, and I ran outside. It was already late morning. The Albanians stood in front of the house with two young priests who'd walked from Genoa with a group of sick and exhausted Italian prisoners. The Albanians had found them in the meadow when the priests stopped to say Mass. The Italians said that the Red Army was a day's march from Löwendorf. Gangs of citizens were in the nearby towns, looking for Americans and Englishmen who'd escaped from prison camps. An RAF pilot who'd parachuted from his burning plane had been beaten to death in a nearby field, and two Löwendorf men were wearing the pilot's leather jacket, fleece cap, and boots.

When the Italians left, Felix asked me to walk to the gates to determine if it was safe to use the road. I looked for Caspar, but couldn't find him—no one had seen him since the previous evening. I wondered if he'd gone to the village to find his mother. Felix had told him to bring her to the Pavilion for safety. As I hurried down the avenue, I could already hear the high-pitched screams of women and children and the moans of frightened animals. I knew from the wireless that hundreds of thousands of refugees and soldiers were on the roads, but I was not prepared for what I saw—nothing could have prepared me.

A man carrying a dead dog shouted as he ran past that enemy tanks were at the crossroad. German soldiers, many of them wounded and without their guns, pushed their way through the crowd, kicking and punching. Lost and abandoned children ran screaming back and forth. Women with suitcases strapped to their backs pushed handcarts heavy with children and small animals. Drunken men and women sang and danced. A horse fell dead in its traces, and three men surrounded it and hacked it to pieces, the crowd fighting over the meat. Young men with bayonets robbed those few refugees who looked as if they might have something to steal. Belongings no longer of value to anyone—a birdcage, a pram missing its wheels—were kicked up and down the road. I searched the crowd for Herr Elias, but it was impossible to make out faces. The hedgerows were white with dust, and it was difficult to breathe.

A line of emaciated men and women, walking two abreast, passed in front of me, prodded by a handful of nervous guards. Many of the prisoners, wearing the remnants of yellow stars on their rags, could barely walk. Two women staggered past the gate, their skeletal arms hanging at their sides. One of them turned toward me, her face absolved of all thought—to my confusion, I felt an overwhelming revulsion—and a guard kicked her to hurry her along. When she stumbled, he raised his rifle and shot her. I took a step toward her, and the guard swung around to point his rifle at me. The others kept walking, their expressions unchanged as the guard stepped over the woman's body and came toward me.

I turned and ran up the drive, stopping when I reached the pump in the yard to pour a bucket of water over my head, and then another, the water running into my eyes and mouth and down my neck. When I at last opened my eyes, I saw Felix, standing with some men I recognized as German soldiers. They were tall, and they wore boots, jodhpurs, and long underwear, having thrown away their weapons and the rest of their uniforms. Felix had given them what clothes he could find, and they politely waited in line to shake his hand before hurrying across the park—they knew not to use the roads—carrying fishing hats, quilted shooting vests, and the striped silk waistcoats Felix liked to wear to weddings.

The villagers did not know whether to stay in their houses or to run away (for the first time in years they greeted me with calls of "*Guten tag, Fräulein,*" rather than the Nazi salute). As it was too late to escape, surrounded as we were on all sides, Felix tried to calm them. They would do whatever Felix told them to do. Intimidated by years of propaganda and the threat of punishment, it was the first time they'd allowed themselves to consider that the war was lost and that their lives were in danger. Felix told them that he would not abandon them. He said that the rumor that Red Army soldiers raped women was undoubtedly exaggerated, and he asked them to return to their homes. He, at least, hoped to finish his breakfast before the Russians arrived, as he assumed they would be hungry. Yes, yes, the men said, you're right, Herr Metzenburg, there is nothing to do. The men gathered their families and went home, knowing that the end of the world was upon them.

The Albanians had brought with them a letter they'd written in Russian, attesting that Felix had been like a father to them and humbly beseeching the Russians to grant him and the village every consideration. They asked Felix to attach it to the front of the Pavilion, and together they solemnly nailed the letter to the door, the rest of us watching in silence. The Albanians were leaving immediately for their country. They said that with the victory of Russia, the Resistance would be busier than ever. They had a last drink with Felix and asked for his blessing. Their departure frightened me more than the news that the Russians would soon be in Löwendorf.

Dorothea's lament about dread and remorse was always in my mind, and I hurried to Caspar's room, fighting my way past the refugees, who were running in and out of the stables. The footman's doeskin breeches that he'd worn to serve at Christmas lunch that first winter of the war were hanging on the back of the door with his ice skates. I sat on his bed. I was wet from my dousing at the pump, and water dripped onto the floor and bare mattress. His radio was gone. I wondered if he'd fled in the certainty that the advancing Russians would take him prisoner—they wouldn't believe that he wasn't a soldier, even with his maimed hand, and perhaps because of it. I lowered my head to his pillow, but it was filled with straw and made me sneeze. I wiped my face and hurried back to the yard.

Despite Felix's reassurances, the refugees in the stables had succumbed to panic. The small planes, which were Russian scouts, buzzed overhead, children screamed, dogs howled, men quarreled. And in the distance, there was the low and unfamiliar bark of the approaching tanks.

I gathered the few pieces of food that I could find. I looked for the smoked jerky that a farmer had traded us for a tire—I suspected that it was donkey meat and wouldn't touch it at first, until I was finally defeated by hunger, even if it was Zara that I was eating—but it was gone. Dorothea's chest of medicines was empty, but I found a small bottle of comfrey tincture, a jar of Saint-John's-wort oil, and some aspirin. I still had half a bottle of the pine needles in alcohol that I used on my hands. I put the knife that Caspar had given me for my birthday in a rucksack, along with a blanket, dish towels, and some cotton wool. I thought about asking Dorothea to help me, but she seemed to be verging on madness. Kreck wasn't able to carry an injured man from the Night Wood, and Roeder was too weak. There was only Felix, who was sickly. I couldn't ask him to abandon the cares of the village to tend to one American soldier. Besides, I reasoned, the man was my own secret. My own treasure. Perhaps I was verging on madness, too.

It took me some time to reach the wood, shivering in my damp clothes, worried that one of the Russian scouts in the observer planes would see me—Dorothea swore that one of them had smiled and tipped his hand to her as he flew back and forth over the park. I rode past the *Fasanerie* where Dorothea's mother had once kept golden pheasants, long overgrown with brambles and weeds. It would make a good hiding place for Werewolves, and I increased my speed. Flashes of gunfire were visible in the trees across the river, and I could hear the hollow boom of distant explosions. I hid the bicycle in the withies once used by the women to make baskets and entered the forest, moving quietly so as not to be seen by anyone lurking in the woods.

"I told you I'd come," I whispered when I as last reached him.

He opened his eyes. There was a smell of urine over the damp smell of earth and pine tar and decaying leaves. "Did you?" His voice was low, and I had to lean close in order to hear him. His forehead was wet with perspiration. "I don't remember that. Can you get me out of this?" He smiled in embarrassment.

The coat was heavy with blood and urine, and I threw it into the bushes. He said that his arm was numb, and I rubbed it. Animals had eaten the candle and the matches, and my little knife was gone. I found the bottle of water in my sack and held his head so that he could drink. "I want to clean your wound."

He shook his head.

"I have a carrot for you. I don't think you have any idea what it is worth."

He smiled as if he knew exactly what it was worth. "Maybe in a minute," he said.

I took out the food I'd brought—a boiled duck's egg, two prunes, the carrot. He ate only a few bites of the egg, and when he'd had enough, turned his head to the side, his lips closed tight, like a child. Perhaps it was the smell of his leg, but he had no interest in food, and I put it aside. I held four aspirin in my palm, and he licked them from my hand, his tongue dry on my skin.

I forced myself to look at his leg. The rag, soaked with pus and blood, was stuck to the wound. I thought that I might be sick. I wanted him to think that I knew what I was doing. I didn't want him to know that I was afraid, and I took a quick drink of water. "I'll have to clean it," I said briskly. "I've brought something for it." I pulled the stopper from the bottle of alcohol. There was a strong smell of raw spirits. I placed my hand over his groin and tipped the bottle over his leg. He didn't scream, but his body convulsed with such agony that I was thrown across his chest, spilling what remained in the bottle.

For a moment, the smell of spirits was stronger than the reek of rotting flesh. I righted myself and, taking a breath, slowly peeled the rag from his leg. I cleaned the wound, using all of the cotton wool, then stood and pulled down my flannel slip and used that, too. I poured the Saint-John's-wort oil over his thigh and wrapped his leg in six linen dish towels bearing the small red monogram FvM. I covered him with the blanket.

"If that doesn't do it," he at last said.

I had the sudden fear that he would try to escape if I left him. "I can't leave you here," I said. I crawled behind him and hooked my forearms under his armpits and tried to raise him. I could smell his skin and his rotting flesh and the urine, and it made me happy. How strange, I thought. How bold and brazen of me. I gave another tug, and he sat up for a moment before tumbling onto his side, taking me with him.

"That's all right," I whispered, my arm caught beneath him. "We'll find a way."

He rolled into my arms. "Who are you?" he asked, not without humor. "You speak English."

"I'm Irish," I said. "I wondered if you might be, too. I can't tell."

He touched his head. "How would you know? No hair, no nothing." He smiled. "I'm from the U.S. of A. A wop from Rhode Island." At my look of confusion, he said, "Italian. Catholic, like you."

I told him that my name was Beatrice. He said that Beatrice didn't sound like an Irish name, and I agreed. He asked if I had a cigarette. I told him I'd bring some the next day. He put his arms around me. I could feel his breath on my face. His mouth did not smell of death, but the sweet smell of resin, and I wondered if he'd been eating pine needles. There was the sound of gunfire nearby. The horizon, I knew, would be blazing with fire. I kissed him.

"Did I tell you our nickname for them was the Goons?" he asked after a while. "They were mostly old men. They wore big straw shoes that stuck out from under their pants. It was the funniest thing I ever saw. I figured it had to be for warmth—who'd wear straw duck's feet if he didn't have to? You could tell their uniforms were stolen from dead Russians—even old men Germans are taller than Russians.

"The camp was for Allied pilots. The Goons thought the pilots were gods. To tell you the truth, we all did. The Goons assigned us to the pilots as orderlies—nothing too personal or too un-American, just cleaning latrines and some light sweeping. A little cooking. We'd been captured near Salerno and shipped across the border in cattle cars. All any of us wanted, even the pilots, was water and salt. Not smokes, but salt. And we wanted to escape. In the beginning, it's all we thought about. It kept us busy day and night, thinking about salt and planning our escape."

He began to cry, and I held him closer.

"Every week, we had a different talk—one of the pilots was from Scotland Yard and another was a history teacher at a big university. The talks were pretty interesting, especially the one on Richard the Lionheart. And the Croydon Airport robbery. It made me think about what I'll do when the war is over— I mean other than putting my nose to work. I figure maybe I'll go back to school."

I waited for him to continue, not wanting him to stop. I thought of the number of times I'd been held in my life. Once or twice by my father. Never by my mother. Herr Elias when we danced in the library. Once by Caspar when I fell on the ice. "What happened then?" I asked.

"We found watchmaking tools in one of the Red Cross boxes. Just what we needed. But it turned out Jimmy's old man was a clock maker, and he knew all about watches. The commandant heard about it and brought him his nice Swiss watch to fix, and soon the guards asked him to fix other things, too. That got us a little extra food."

He drifted in and out of consciousness. Once he began to shout, and I rocked him gently until he stopped. He shifted his body to ease the pain, his head against my breast. "It won't be long now," he whispered. "Don't forget me."

"Never," I said.

We were warm in our little bower, nestled in the leaves. A red fox stopped to stare at us over its shoulder, perhaps drawn by the smell of blood, then turned disdainfully and disappeared in the brush. An owl settled on a branch, ruffling its wings impatiently as it found its perch. A blind vole scuttled past my feet. The whole forest seemed to be moving, not only foxes (there were no rabbits left in Germany), but high above us, even the sky swayed and burned. I sang to him one of the songs that Felix liked to play on the gramophone while he dressed until I, too, fell asleep.

It was near dawn when his voice woke me, and I wondered if he'd been talking all night. "It was the start of spring," he said. "It wasn't so damn cold anymore. We were shaken the hell out of our bunks. The Reds were only a day's march away, and the camp was shutting down. We started walking, even though it was the middle of the night, stopping only when the Goons couldn't take another step, giving them, God help us, a chance to rest. There were five hundred of us and twenty of them, but when one of the boys tried to sneak away, a guard shot him dead."

He motioned for some water, and I held his head so he could drink. He said that he had no feeling in his leg, and the pain was a little better. "We found some half rations left in a church by the Red Cross, most of them rotten, but we ate them anyway. Some of the men were puking and crapping in the snow, and I felt sorry for them—they couldn't help it if they ate everything at once. One of the English pilots said he could see the fires in Berlin, but he was only imagining it—he'd already spotted Hitler twice that morning.

"The first night, about thirty of us slept in a shed in the middle of a field—the others squeezed into a deserted farmhouse and some barns. There was nothing in the shed, not even windows, only a few cow bones and an empty water trough. In the morning when we went outside, everyone was gone. We couldn't believe it! We celebrated with instant iced coffee, made with a couple of coffee crystals one of the officers had hidden in his pocket. When we calmed down, we realized we had no place to go—we didn't even know where we were—and we hurried down the road after them. Now and then we'd pass a burning house, and we'd stand close to the fire for a few minutes to get warm. We figured thirty of us could move faster than hundreds of them, and once in a while we saw traces of them—a canteen with my friend's name and some RAF flight maps the pilots had saved—but we couldn't catch up with them, and we wondered if maybe they'd turned off the road. We could hear explosions and tank fire, and sometimes even shouting, and from then on we stuck to cattle trails. Sometimes we saw a group of men hurrying through the woods, or a family with their animals, but we all acted as if we were invisible, even the cows. When we stopped that night, I just kept going. No one even noticed, but no one would've cared, either. Who was going to stop me?

"After walking for about an hour, I saw a high stone wall with a pair of fancy iron gates hanging from their hinges. The sound of gunfire was louder, and I could tell there was a road nearby. I could hear people shouting and running. I ducked inside the gates. Trees were planted in two long rows with a sandy road in the middle, and I knew there'd be a nice house at the end of it. I could smell stewed fruit, maybe apricots, which made me worry for a minute maybe I was hallucinating, like the English pilot. My nose again!

"I saw the burned walls of what must've been a big mansion once. There were some other buildings nearby and a yard with a clock tower, but no people. No lights. I was figuring what to do next when there was a flash and then a rifle shot. I knew I was hit, even though I'd heard stories about being shot and not realizing it 'til your boot was full of blood. I heard a low whistle, and suddenly men were coming through the trees. I started to run. It wasn't easy. I'd been shot in the leg, and I had to keep stopping." He smiled. "The next thing I knew, a girl was trying to bury me."

It was early morning when I left him. Smoke drifted through the woods, and I could hear heavy artillery fire (Caspar had taught me the difference between the sound of a howitzer and that of an antitank gun). As I turned into the park, I smelled gasoline.

Two tanks were rolling across the lawn. Naked men were in the river, splashing and shouting. A Russian lorry was parked in the yard. Soldiers were in the kitchen garden, kicking through the dirt as they searched for roots to eat. Some of them wore women's hats and shawls, and one held a parasol over his head.

There was an explosion—the retreating German army blowing up a bridge, perhaps—and although the explosion must have been a quarter of a mile away, I threw myself to the ground. I lay there, hands over my head, waiting for the next explosion, but none came. The soldiers standing around the lorry laughed and waved as I got to my feet.

Felix was in front of the Pavilion with a Russian officer and his men. Although Felix spoke Russian, he listened patiently, leaning on a stick, as a smiling man in the striped jacket of a prisoner of war translated for the Russians. The officer, discerning from Felix's expression that he understood Russian, turned aside the translator and apologized to Felix, speaking to him directly as he folded the Albanians' letter attesting to Felix's goodwill and buttoned it inside his breast pocket.

Dorothea and Kreck stood in the doorway of the stables with the Black Sea women and children, some refugees I'd never seen before, and the Frenchmen. The interpreter waved to the children gaily, calling in German, then in Polish, but they did not move or change expression.

Felix went into the house with the officer. When they returned, the officer saluted Felix, and he and his men climbed into the lorry. The tanks had uprooted many of the elms in the avenue, and the lorry appeared intermittently in the gaps between the trees. In the park, the soldiers who'd been left behind dried themselves after their bath, gesturing to the women and waving cigarettes, but the women refused to look at them. Felix explained that the Russians had come to requisition the house for one of their generals. As there was no armistice yet, the tanks and the soldiers would remain in the park, where the trees would conceal them until the war had officially ended. He said that the general and his staff would be at the Pavilion in an hour.

I followed Dorothea into the house, where Roeder was already packing. Dorothea, indecisive before a journey, put on three sweaters, then pulled them impatiently over her head. She put on the trousers I'd made for her, a polka-dot shirt, and a tweed hacking jacket. I ran to empty my workbasket, throwing two sweaters into a suitcase, along with a shawl, Felix's flannel trousers, a pencil, and my journal. When I returned to Dorothea's room, Felix, his arms full of books, stood watching as Dorothea, wearing a black Persian-lamb bolero made for her by Schiaparelli, studied herself in a mirror.

"I don't believe you'll need that, darling," he said smoothly. She looked at him.

"Charming as it is."

"I'm preparing for all seasons," she said with a giddy smile as he helped Roeder to fit some bath soap and Dorothea's gold brushes into a bag.

"By the way," he asked, "where are we going?"

"To the forest," Dorothea said, surprised that he should wonder. "To the Night Wood. There's no other place for us. We'll hide in Grandfather's clearing." There was something bright and brittle about her that alarmed me, and I saw that Felix, too, was concerned. He kissed her, and I realized that it was the first time I'd seen them kiss.

We carried our suitcases into the yard. There were even more strangers, and I wondered how their number had grown so quickly in the few minutes we'd been in the Pavilion. Convinced that they could use the old carriages, even though there were no horses, the men had pulled an old victoria into the yard and had begun loading it. When it was at last admitted that they could not possibly pull the heavy carriage, the bedding and sacks and children and old women were lifted down from the carriage and passed by hand to small carts and wagons.

Roeder, most practical of all, grabbed cooking pots and whatever food was left in the cellar, and with the help of Lazare and Maxime loaded them onto a cart. Felix asked Kreck to see that two straw chairs from the kitchen garden were not forgotten ("That way, we won't have to sit on the wet ground"), and the chairs sat precariously atop a mound of disordered bundles. The refugees ran in and out of the stables, brushing past the curious Russian soldiers, many of whom wore five and six wristwatches, some of them women's watches. A young soldier opened one of Dorothea's bags to rummage through it, slowly selecting objects that caught his fancy and putting them in his pockets—a cigarette case, the gold brushes, a pair of sunglasses, a dog collar. He wrapped a silk scarf around his neck.

When I noticed that Felix had stopped to watch the soldier, I took him by the arm, suggesting that we look one last time in the house—we might have forgotten something. He turned to me with a knowing smile, and we walked to the house with Dorothea, Bresla, and Madame Tkvarcheli. As we stood in the drawing room, a soldier who'd been roaming through the house came unsteadily through the door, a revolver in one hand and a bottle of schnapps in the other. Another soldier, an older man, wandered into the room after him. As we turned to leave, the first soldier, swaying back and forth, gestured at Felix. "No men!" he shouted in German. *"Keine Männer!"* When Felix did not move, the soldier grabbed him by the collar and shoved him roughly into the hall, locking the door behind him.

The soldier dragged an armchair to the fireplace, where he sat himself with a contented grunt, grinning in amazement at his good fortune. He gestured to Bresla to come to him, and when she did not move, he squinted one eye and playfully aimed his gun at her. She cursed and ducked behind a table, which seemed only to increase his good humor. He called to his friend, who was in the dining room loading his pockets with silver, and the man peeked around the door to shout his encouragement.

Madame Tkvarcheli, pale with fear, fell to her knees to beg the soldier's forgiveness. I could hear Felix's voice over the curses and pleas of Bresla and her mother. Dorothea slipped off her watch and offered it to the soldier, her hand shaking. The Russian sighed in exasperation and rose from his chair. As he reached to grab Bresla, I stepped between them. The soldier, pleasantly surprised, looked at me appraisingly, then, with a satisfied smile, raised the gun to my mouth, grabbed Dorothea's watch, and, to the delight of his friend, pushed me into the dining room.

The shutters had been drawn, and the room was dark. The carpet was strewn with the contents of the silver drawers, and the soldier cursed as he tripped over a champagne bucket. I was wearing four sweaters and a wool skirt over my trousers and, to their frustration, it took some time to strip away my clothes. They smelled of alcohol, and the fingernails of the younger man were ragged and sharp. As they pushed me back and forth between them, pulling my trousers to my ankles, my mind began to wander. As a child, I'd been told by my mother that a girl would die instantly if she had sexual intercourse before her first period, and I wondered if you would also die if you no longer menstruated. For a moment, I was able to conjure the face of Mr. Knox (and quickly erased it, not wanting him to see me).

When I began to cry, the old man punched me in the face, ordering me to shut my Hun mouth. It did not take very long, once they realized that I was a virgin and used one of Frau Schumacher's forks to pierce me. When they finished, they wiped themselves on the tablecloth and left through the kitchen, taking as much silver as they could carry and my shoes and clothes. I tried to stand, but my legs would not hold me. I crawled to the door, rising to my knees to draw the bolt. The door swung open, and I fell into the room.

The women cleaned me as best they could, as ceremonious as the handmaidens of a bride, and dressed me in pieces of their clothing. Dorothea removed her sweater and pulled my arms through its sleeves. Madame Tkvarcheli gave me her shawl, and Bresla tied her apron around my waist. They carried me from the house. The Russians watched us, some of them laughing. The two drunken soldiers were at the pump, arguing over a soup tureen and one of my sweaters. Felix took me from the women and lifted me shakily onto one of the wagons as it began to rain. I remembered that first day in Berlin when he'd warned me that he could not offer me his protection, and I wondered if he remembered it, too.

The refugees followed the wagons, pushing wheelbarrows and pulling carts laden with blankets and pots. A silver sled, once used by Dorothea and her governess, was loaded with children, and the Frenchmen dragged it after them, the bells on the sled ringing gaily. As we crossed the park, more people began to appear—escaped prisoners of war, Polish and Belgian and Dutch slave workers, farmers from the burned towns nearby, city people, and German soldiers. When we reached the edge of the wood, the men unloaded the wagons and sled, people carrying whatever they could bear. A man hoisted me onto his back, and Dorothea led us into the forest.

It was not easy, moving along the dark and overgrown path. The excited dogs lunged back and forth, causing the children to cry, and the burdens were cumbersome and heavy. My head hurt. I wondered if I'd been turned into a parrot. I wondered if I'd been beaten with an iron rod for refusing to speak.

It was two days before I was myself again. Dorothea said that she had feared for my life, if not my mind. I had persisted, she said, in claiming that I'd hidden my lover, an American, in the Night Wood. I'd also told her that I was a parrot whose name was Beatrice.

"There is an American in the woods," I said. "And my name is Beatrice." My head throbbed, and there was a burning between my legs. I watched as Roeder soaked herbs in a dish of water, pulling the leaves apart with her hands. It was the first time I'd seen her bare hands, and they were white and slender. Dorothea, who had torn her polka-dot shirt to make bandages, gestured to me to turn on my side. "That your cuts are not more infected is thanks to Roeder," she said. When I apologized for the stench of my body, she looked irritated. "You can't smell," she said, looking at Roeder, who shook her head. "Your nose is broken."

Any delicacy that once served to safeguard our modesty had vanished, and they worked efficiently and without embarrassment. I, too, a virginal girl, at least in spirit, was without shame, at least in those first days, perhaps because I felt nothing at all. The bitter medicine made from willow bark seemed to calm me, the pain no longer so piercing.

I lay on a blanket on the ground, listening to the sound of the fire as it gained and lost strength, the flames bright against the dark forest. The quiet talk of the women, speaking in many languages, was soothing, as were the cries of the birds, also in many languages. I did not mention the American dying in the woods—it angered Dorothea if I spoke of him. One night, I managed to crawl a few yards from my blanket before Bessie heard me and began to bark, alerting Felix, who sent me back to bed with a scolding.

On the third day, Dorothea allowed me to go to the latrine on my own. It was painful to walk and I made several wrong turnings before I found him. He lay facedown in the leaves, not far from where I'd left him. My flannel slip was wrapped around his neck. His blackened thigh, swarming with maggots, was swollen to twice its size, and his feet and arms were marked with the bites and scratches of animals. One of his ears had been eaten away.

I knelt beside him and put my fingers on his neck. As I opened his mouth to breathe into it, I heard someone call my name.

Caspar, thin and pale, a ragged blanket around his shoulders, stepped from behind a tree. His face was both swollen and withered, and his sparse growth of blond beard made him look older. He glanced at my legs, streaked with blood, and at my broken nose, and gave me his hand, pulling me to my feet. He drank the water I'd brought, and we folded his blanket into a sling and gently rolled the American to the center of it.

Caspar, walking backward, made an opening in the briar, the dry branches snapping noisily around us. I needed to rest, and I gestured to him to stop. When I leaned over the American to wipe his face, I heard shouting. Men were running on the path. Caspar looked around in alarm, and I felt the full weight of the blanket. I reached for him, but I was blinded by the gunfire, and I could not find him.

They washed and wrapped his body, and Felix and the Frenchmen carried the American into the woods, where he was buried, I was told, in a grave lined with moss and ferns. My delirium had returned, and I was not allowed to go with them.

Caspar slept next to me on the ground, his arm and chest bandaged in what was left of Dorothea's polka-dot shirt. The Polish surgeon who'd examined him said that the bullet had only grazed his shoulder. He would soon be well again—ready to kill some Russians, the doctor said. He'd been shot by men looking for the half ton of gold Felix was said to have brought from Löwendorf.

He told me that he'd been with a small company of men determined to fight the Russians. They'd been betrayed, and he'd escaped with a friend, but they'd been separated. He was on his way to meet his friend when he came upon me in the woods. He'd heard rumors of a camp in the clearing. He'd also heard that the Russians had taken me away with them.

I apologized to him for my smell, and he said, "You smell like pine trees." When I was silent, he said, "I know. Kreck told me." He turned so that he was resting on his good side. It had rained that day, and his shoulder ached. "It doesn't make any difference. What happened in the Pavilion." He stretched alongside me, our heads on one blanket.

I didn't know what to say. I hadn't considered that what had happened to me would make a difference to anyone but myself. My own revulsion was quite sufficient.

"I wish we were fishing," he said. "I don't know how you do it. Maybe you are a trout yourself. When this is over, I want you to teach me. Other things, too. How to speak English. How to dance."

"I don't know how to dance," I said. I thought of Herr Elias and the way that his body had felt, pressed against mine, and I thought of the Russian soldiers, and I began to cry.

Caspar held his mouth to my ear, whispering that he was going to fight the Russians with tricks only a poacher would know. He said that his sister, dyed as red as a macaw, had been killed at Sachsenhausen. One of his brothers had died at Danzig, and the other, the Communist, had died in Buchenwald. I held his hands and kissed them. Sometime in the middle of the night, I fell asleep in his arms. When I awoke in the morning, he was gone.

. . .

My body began to heal, as bodies tend to do, whether you want them to or not. In a week's time, I could urinate without too much pain, although I still could not breathe through my nose. At night, Roeder sang the songs she remembered from her youth with unexpected tenderness and even longing ("When We Are Married" was a favorite). It had never occurred to me that Roeder could sing, and I wondered what else I had missed. Hearing her voice, the refugees sometimes sang songs of their own, songs from Hungary, Latvia, and Moldavia. Although I didn't understand the words, I knew that the songs were always about love or berries. Sometimes both.

One of the women had hidden a pregnant cat in a basket, and others had carried their canaries. A few of the men had been followed by their dogs, and the dogs, which had been scavenging on the roads for corpses, looked happy and full. Felix had brought the sack of Ethiopian coffee and a coffee mill, along with two tins of biscuits and the last case of sardines in tomato sauce. After careful calculation, he concluded that there was sufficient coffee (half a cup) for each person, including the children, for sixteen days. With the arrival each day, however, of more refugees and travelers, he was constantly obliged to redo his figures (as people arrived in the clearing, others disappeared), and these calculations gave him many hours of distraction. He divided the coffee with the same care he'd once taken with his treasure map.

I knew that I was succumbing to the sin of pride to imagine that I was to blame for the American's death. If I'd been able to return to the Night Wood as I'd promised, if I had told Felix and Dorothea, rather than holding my secret close to me, if I had confided in Caspar that night when we drank champagne in the drawing room, if I had not cherished my girlish dreams of love and romance, if I had not read and, what is worse, believed all of those novels, if I had stayed in Ballycarra, if I had never taught myself to make lace. My list—no longer ivory boxes and fox collars—was endless.

I was given charge of the noisy band of children, partly to keep them from tormenting Kreck (he'd lost his monocle, and his puckered eye socket provoked the children to screams of terror) and also, I suspected, to keep me busy. I took them into the forest for a few hours each day, Maxime and Bertrand accompanying us for safety, where we collected roots and herbs. We stripped the bark from the Wych elms for the women to grind into powder (it didn't taste too bad, although my bowels turned to water), and we picked licorice fern and the delicious Queen Anne's lace.

Mr. Knox particularly admired the book *At Swim-Two-Birds*, and I thought of it as we walked along. *The lamenting of a wounded otter in a black hole, sweeter than harpstrings that. There is no torture so narrow as to be bound and beset in a dark cavern without food or music, without the bestowing of gold on bards. To be chained by night in a dark pit without company of chessmen—evil destiny!* The words went pleasantly, ceaselessly, through my head as I led the children through the woods. Despite my dislike of catching birds, I taught them to make Caspar's ingenious bird trap, which provided us with an occasional treat. We roasted the birds on spits as soon as we caught them, happily complicit in our desire not to share the birds with the others.

At night, when the news and rumors of the day had at last been exhausted, and the women had soothed the hungry children, and Dorothea had fallen asleep in the straw garden chair, a book open on her chest, I struggled to understand all that had happened. Not simply what had happened to me, but what had happened to all of us. I knew what others had suffered.

Kreck estimated that the camp's supplies, even with the food contributed by newcomers, would not last more than six days. The impassioned talk about the future soon lost its immediacy once we finished the last of the potatoes, burning the stalks and roasting them in the fire. The newcomers shared what they had—a duck, or a bottle of schnapps made from beech leaves, or a small piece of meat (I'd grown to like horse meat)—but there was not enough food to feed everyone. There had been forty of us that first night in the rain, but the camp had grown to almost a hundred people.

The camp had begun to spread into the forest itself—different families, and then clans, and even countries claiming certain areas for themselves. The Sudetenland Germans settled as far as possible from the Czechs. The Ukrainians claimed the beech wood, while the few Jews, like the deserters, were scattered deep in the forest. The children, who quickly learned the borders of each neighborhood, some of the refugees more welcoming than others, tended to stay in their own territory when they were not roaming through the forest.

With the arrival of new refugees came more news and rumors. Goebbels had poisoned Hitler and his new wife, Eva Braun, in their cement submarine, and then shot himself. Admiral Dönitz was appointed president of Germany. Göring was hiding in his castle in Veldenstein, protected by nine drugged parachute divisions. Some of the rumors were incredible (the English had made a deal with the Russians, allowing them to take Berlin; the commandant at Sachsenhausen had ordered his prisoners onto barges that were then sunk in the Baltic Sea), but that did not stop us from believing them.

Dorothea and Felix sat as king and queen in the center of it all, not requiring or even desiring their suzerainty, tirelessly dispensing food, clothing, and advice (some of the refugees angrily refused to believe Felix when he told them that their money was worthless). That the Metzenburgs were the commissars of a community run on socialist principles, despite the quickly established borders, amused them in its irony and even compelled them to admit that as a simple system it had much to admire.

The weather at last turned warm, and the magnolia and chestnut trees came into bud. There were bright leaves on the acacias. Under the trees, the dame's violet leapt into long pods, curving toward the light as it awaited its flowers. (Dame's violet, Dorothea had once told me, is a garden escape, an idea that had made me smile.) My head was still too heavy for me to read, but Dorothea, studying the book of Chinese history Felix had brought with him, sometimes read aloud to me. I traded a spool of horsehair for a pair of mouse-lined slippers and a needle with a Hungarian woman, both of us delighted by our shrewd bartering skills.

With the fear of starvation came other fears. Some of the deserters spoke of the Charlemagne Battalion, a group of fighters composed of SS men and fanatics from across Europe who fancied themselves the new Crusaders, an exclusive cult of warriors who would be the last defense against the Asian barbarians steadily edging their way across the continent. The men vowed to keep fighting even when there was an armistice, and there had been reports of them in the woods south of Berlin. I hoped that Caspar hadn't joined the Charlemagne Battalion.

Felix, who'd been feeling low, asked me one morning to shave him. It was a task that Kreck would customarily have performed in the absence of Caspar, but Kreck's crippled fingers made him a dangerous barber. Felix handed me a crude razor he'd laboriously fashioned from a broken knife blade and a piece of wood and calmly rested his head on the back of his chair. The razor was unsteady in its improvised binding, but he did not flinch. I drew the blade back and forth across his face, the knife making a harsh sound as it scraped against his dry skin. Kreck watched solemnly as I worked. "*Sei vorsichtig, das ist seine empfindlichste Stelle!*" he shouted, pointing with a shaking finger. Be careful, that is his delicate spot! Felix's face was bright red when I finished, and there were two small nicks, but his beard was gone. Although we had no mirror, he said that he could tell just by touch that I'd done a finer job than his barber in Berlin.

· · ·

Dorothea had once resented it if even one of the trees in her grandfather's wood was cut, but since the beginning of the war, she'd allowed anyone to enter the forest to take whatever wood he needed. As Dorothea and I left camp one morning to cut wood, accompanied by two Latvians who would actually do the work, Felix said, "The best fires, of course, are those made with ash. Pine and fir burn too quickly, as I'm sure you know." I looked at him in astonishment—I should have known that he even had an opinion about firewood. I took it as a further sign that he was feeling better.

In deference to Felix, an ash was chosen, and the Latvians made a good cut before they began to saw in earnest. The axe was heavy, and it was not easy to find the mark each time. The wood was moist, and the saw stuck in the wood, but after an hour of sawing—the men took turns and were eventually able to use a rusty two-handed saw—the tree began to sway hesitantly. The branches were entangled with the trees surrounding it, which seemed to bend toward it in support, but it was too late, and with a last shudder and groan, the tree fell to the ground. I, who had done nothing, was too exhausted to speak.

The children met us when we returned to camp, the wagon piled with wood, watching as the logs were arranged in a pyramid. Kreck and Felix watched, too, waiting patiently for the fire to catch. Dorothea, who'd been punished as a child for setting fires with the flints she found in the park, was good at making fires, even with damp spring wood. She'd carried one of her boxes of flints with her when we left the Pavilion, comforted, she said, by the knowledge that the flints, imprinted with centipedes and seashells, were millions of years old. She used one of her flints to light the wood, but it was too green, even for Dorothea, and refused to burn.

Felix calculated that we'd been in the Night Wood for sixteen days. There was enough food for two more days.

That night, as I ran back and forth to the latrine, I had the strange feeling that something had changed. It was impossible to grasp hold of it. As the night wore on, however, it slowly came to me that I could no longer hear the faint drone of tanks or the intermittent rattle of machine-gun fire. I didn't know how to account for it, the overwhelming relief of it, and I decided that I was suffering another trick of my weakened mind.

I was awakened near morning by cries of jubilation. Women took up pot lids, banging them loudly, and some of the men did somersaults, causing the children to cry. Kreck danced shakily with Dorothea, while Felix, overcome, fell into his chair, his hands over his face. The man who came with the news was making his third tour of the camp, borne on the shoulders of some Belgian prisoners of war. Berlin had capitulated to the Red Army. Hitler was dead. The Americans were entering the city from the west.

There frequently had been rumors of the war's end, and we had learned not to believe them, but the empty sky, the cease of gunfire, the silence of the forest itself, told us that the news was true. The war was over. The feeling of shock was so great that for several hours all that we could do was run back and forth through the camp, embracing one another and crying. I found Bresla and the Odessa women and we prayed and sang together, the women holding me in their arms.

In the afternoon, a man from the village came to tell Felix that the Russian general and his staff had left Löwendorf. He said there'd been talk that the Metzenburgs had abandoned the Pavilion. At this news, Dorothea and Felix decided to return at once. We began to collect our few things, but Kreck, assuring Felix that he and Roeder would soon follow, urged him to leave immediately. Accompanied by Bessie, we set out for home.

The hawthorn was in bloom. Blue herons paced tentatively along the river's edge, and there even were bees. I saw two waxwings in the willows, lurking like thieves, black masks over their brown eyes. Mr. Knox had once told me that waxwings were very confiding, and I wondered what stories they would have to tell me.

Although the general and his staff were gone, one of the tanks and some of the soldiers remained in a disorderly encampment. Clouds of flies, attracted by the stench of rotting flesh, swarmed over the river, its surface marked by astonished trout. Dorothea's collection of eighteenth-century books, among them prints of frogs and toads from Catesby's *Natural History*, was scattered across the park, and the frogs, flying across the torn pages, looked as if they were alive. Strips of carpet hung from the trees, and the ground was strewn with broken porcelain and pieces of painted canvas (I saw the face of Dorothea's mother on one of them). The windows and doors of the Pavilion had been smashed, and mounds of broken glass and brick were piled high around the house. We had expected much worse.

In the yard, Frau Blucher from the inn, wearing a blue velvet hat and the jacket of a Lanvin suit, a bit too small for her, was busy trading a soldier a bottle of schnapps for one of Dorothea's teapots.

"I would tell you that you'll have another Lanvin if I thought it mattered to you," Felix said to Dorothea. I'd noticed that once we were out of the Night Wood and in the light again, Felix looked old. He wasn't old, I knew, but his face had a yellow pallor, and I wondered if he had jaundice. Many of the refugees in the camp had been sick.

I followed Felix and Dorothea into the house. A group of Red Army soldiers sprawled on the floor of the drawing room stared at us as if we were unexpected and unwelcome guests. There was a smell of urine, wood smoke, and excrement. Russian words and crude drawings were scratched across the walls. The chairs and sofas had been ripped apart and the stuffing burned. On the bare floor, nearly buried under garbage and waste, were torn books, bed linen, strips of curtain, and broken plates. The gramophone records had been snapped in two, and the gramophone was gone. At the sight of her torn wedding veil, Dorothea looked happy for a moment. "I'd forgotten about my veil," she said. Felix took her hand, and we left the house.

A soldier stood in the doorway of the stables, arguing loudly with a woman who looked like Herr Pflüger's wife, both of them tugging on one of Dorothea's sheets.

"Do you remember when I said that if we loved it, we had to protect it?" Felix asked Dorothea.

"Not likely that I'd forget," she said.

"I'm not sure that we were successful."

We watched in silence as more soldiers, some of them wearing Felix's clothes, joined the argument. Suddenly, the commotion in the yard grew louder.

Coming across the park, a hawthorn stick in his hand, was Kreck, followed by Roeder and a band of drunken and ecstatic refugees. Pipes were played and drums banged as the children twirled and shouted in excitement. Kreck had fashioned an eye patch out of a piece of sacking—he looked like a mountain king, the tips of his overgrown mustache, no longer black, springing from his face. His rusty frock coat, once a little tight across his back, hung loosely from his shoulders. Dogs swirled around him as he stopped in front of the Pavilion and shook his stick in triumph. Not Ovid, I thought, but the Brothers Grimm. We are rat catchers, bewitched swans, witches.

We confined ourselves to the upper floors of the Pavilion, sleeping on straw. We had no candles or oil for lamps, and water had to be carried from the well in the yard. Despite the foul smell of my body, I thought constantly of food. The food was always Irish. Brown bread with butter, salmon, oatmeal with cream, boiled cabbage with bacon (but no potatoes). I used to dream of Herr Elias, but after the war I dreamed of food.

Bresla and her mother chose not to return to Odessa with their friends, and Felix gave them the use of an abandoned farmhouse that he owned in the village. Lazare was taking

Bresla's aunt (she of the Immaculate Conception) with him to France. Bertrand was traveling to Odessa with Bresla's cousin, explaining that he'd pretended to be her husband for so long, he couldn't conceive of life without her. The departure of the Frenchmen and the women and their children made us sad, and Bresla and I walked with them as far as the crossroad.

As there was no telephone service or post, letters continued to arrive mysteriously, passed from hand to hand and village to village, slipped under a door or left at the foot of a tree. I spent two days searching for a pencil, at last finding one at the back of a broken desk drawer. I sharpened it with Felix's home-made razor and wrote to my parents and to Mr. Knox, entrusting the letters to a foreign worker on his way to Belgium.

Most of the people in camp had already started for home, but those who remained were invited to stay in the stables for as long as they wished. They were understandably eager to be on their way, and each day there were fewer of them. We had nothing to eat, and Felix sold two of the motorcars to Herr Pflüger for food.

One morning, the soldiers were gone from the park—Dorothea said that it was thanks to our exhaustion that we neither saw nor heard them leave. They'd retreated only as far as the village, however, coming drunk every day to the Pavilion to demand that Felix tell them where he'd hidden his gold. The villagers did not trouble themselves over vagaries like hidden gold. Herr Pflüger's son, recently returned from the Western

Front, carried away the last pair of firedogs, seven brass door-knobs, and a stuffed owl. Many of the soldiers had never seen a bicycle, and they crashed our bicycles full speed into walls and rode off the bridge into the river. There were fights, and a soldier was shot in a quarrel over a tire pump.

As Löwendorf and other villages south and east of Berlin had been declared part of the new Russian zone of occupation, landowners in the neighborhood were said to be joining the Communist Party as fast as they could find the local commissar. Some Ukrainian refugees who'd been slave workers in Poznan refused to return to Russia, confiding to Bresla that they and their children had been treated brutally by their own soldiers. If a woman raped by a Russian soldier was later found to be pregnant or suffering from venereal disease, she was sent to Siberia. The Ukrainians were determined to reach Canada, and one morning they were gone from the stables.

At the end of May, the Russians drove the tank from the village, careening noisily down the rutted road to a nearby town. The armistice had been signed early in the month, and there was no longer any reason to hide the tank. The soldiers took our bicycles with them, except for one that I'd hidden in the meadow.

Word came that one of the farmers, just returned from the war, had hung himself, and Felix and I walked to his farm. The craters in the road were filled with waste, and we took the path through the orchard. Makeshift shelters had been set up in the fields, and there was a strong smell of sewage. Both of us were still a bit weak, and it took us an hour to reach the farm, eating the apples we'd picked along the way.

The man's body was swinging from a beech, a rough ladder leaning against the tree. His wife stood under the body, staring at his bare feet. She said that the Russian soldiers had destroyed his hives for sport and had used his furniture for shooting practice. He'd not been able to bear the loss of his bees and his grandmother's chairs. Someone, she said, had stolen the shoes from his feet.

Boys from the village cut down the body at Felix's direction. The rope had distended the man's neck, and the distance between his jaw and shoulders was elongated. When Felix bent to help the woman with the body, she spat at him. We left her there, surrounded by the laughing boys. I had to stop twice on the way home, vomiting in the weeds.

A few days later, Dorothea asked me to accompany her to the basement of the Pavilion. The filth left by the soldiers reached our knees (reminding me of Pepys's cellar), and we spent the morning clearing a path to a coal chute in the corner where Dorothea remembered that Caspar had hidden a painting— a small Cranach, she said. Using sticks, we searched in several places, finding three bags containing jewelry and two silver chalices, but no Cranach. "Venus, and Cupid stung by bees," she said, panting with the effort of digging. When she noticed that my hands were shaking, she took my stick from me. "Remember where these are buried," she said as she returned the treasures to their hiding places, which made me wonder if she feared for her memory. Or perhaps, I thought in alarm, she and Felix were leaving Löwendorf and did not intend to take me with them.

It was the beginning of summer. The windows and the roof had not been repaired, and it was possible, if you were not too distracted, to hear the unaccustomed sound of motorcars on the road. There was even the sound of singing now and then. Although thousands of refugees and prisoners of war were still moving across the land, there were fewer than before, and the victorious Allied soldiers seemed to keep to Berlin.

I worried that I would not have the strength to hold on to my happiness (if I still kept lists, my longing to keep at least some small part of it would be at the top). It was difficult to ease my grief, burdened like others with a new and permanent sense of dread. Those moments when I could not help but feel pleasure—eating a fresh egg or finding a book that was not missing its pages—filled me with shame.

I understood that the division of time is determined by astral and lunar phenomena, but I began to wonder if sorrow and elation also have their own tidal and rotational cycles, all part of the encompassing natural world. If Felix's generation suffered death and humiliation in the Great War, we had been left with the inexhaustible presence of evil. That people, including myself, could so easily resume their old ways and habits seemed a repudiation of all that had been lost. I couldn't bear the thought that everything would remain the same, yet I was frightened by the new world that awaited us.

During the war, we had scavenged at night and slept in the day. Children had not gone to school. Animals had not foaled. There'd been no appointments to keep or to cancel, no market days, weddings, or funerals, and no cars, buses, trains, or horses to get us there, had there been someplace to go. There'd been no telephones, electricity, petrol. No medicine. No money and no food.

We had survived, but we were different people.

Dorothea and Felix made no mention of leaving Löwendorf, and I was further relieved when Dorothea asked Bresla and me to help with the restoration of the kitchen garden. Women from the village, who at first watched silently from the garden door, slowly began to offer advice, surprised and pleased to see that we worked as hard and as long as they themselves worked. They brought us seeds and even tools, trading them for a share in the garden. It was too late to plant all of the seeds, but we were in time for tomatoes, snap beans, carrots, and beets, setting them against the east wall where the seedlings would be sheltered from the wind. We mixed dirt with sand from the river to plant parsley and fennel. Advised by the farmers' wives, we chose a day that was dry to plant cabbage and onions. The women, who once believed that the glittering paths of the garden were paved with gold, thanks to the mica in the sand, taught us to sow with the waxing of the moon, and we planted white poppies and hyssop. The little huts in each corner of the garden, made with bent juniper poles and covered with grapevines, had been stripped by the soldiers when they ate the leaves, and I planted a myrrh-scented climbing rose, winding the stems through the lattice. I also planted a cutting of blue honeyberry, which birds like very much.

Madame Tkvarcheli worked in the kitchen—walnuts, soft and green, were just right for pickling, she said. Bresla was learning to speak German, and if I was not too tired, I gave her lessons in the evening. Frau Hoffeldt and Frau Bodenschatz had returned to the village with their children, but they, too, came each day to help in the garden and in the house.

Felix fell ill a few weeks after our return. Although he had a fever, he had no pain or further symptoms of disease. When he refused to eat, Madame Tkvarcheli made nettle tea for him, which she said was a cure for grief. He liked that the leaves resembled the face of a weasel, but he would not touch the tea, and Dorothea and I drank it instead.

One night, I heard Dorothea say to him, "You must never leave me, Felix. I couldn't bear it. You must swear to me. I understand nothing. Not money. Not people, especially Germans. I would be lost without you."

Felix's answer was not very satisfactory. "We've returned to the time of the Great Migrations. All of Europe is in motion. Everything we learned to take for granted is no longer certain—the preservation of knowledge and life without constant fear of death. We'll live like medieval monks, modest and humble in our diligence. That might suit us, darling," he said.

"Suit you, perhaps," she said quietly.

He looked at her in disappointment but said nothing. The possibility that Felix might be wrong was so new to me, so subversive a thought, that I felt myself blush in apology.

Later when she couldn't sleep, Dorothea lit a candle and asked if she could read to me—first in French and then translating the words into English. *That melancholy which we feel when we cease to obey orders which, from one day to another, keep the future hidden, and realise that we have at last begun to live in real earnest, as a grown-up person, the life, the only life that any of us has at his disposal.*

Felix, who we thought was asleep, asked what she was reading. She said that she'd been rereading parts of Proust, having found some torn pages of *Sodom and Gomorrah*, which she'd laboriously pieced together.

He was silent for a moment and then lifted his head. "You must never say that you are 'rereading' Proust, darling. Any knowledgeable person, hearing that you are reading Proust at your age, will know that it is not for the first time." His head fell back on the pillow.

"So much for the monastery," she whispered to me.

Roeder, suffering from a complaint that often left her unable to walk, asked Dorothea if she might return to her own village of Mittelbach, sixty miles from Löwendorf. Her nephew had been killed in the Ardennes, but her brother, a miller, and his wife had survived the war, and he'd sent word that he would welcome her in their home. At the last minute, she didn't want to go, clinging to Dorothea's knees like a child, convinced that Dorothea would die without her. Dorothea told her that she didn't have to go, that she would look after her, and that she had always assumed that they would be old women together.

Wiping her wrinkled face, Roeder looked slowly around the filthy yard, and at the ruins of the Yellow Palace and the looted Pavilion and at Dorothea in her mended men's trousers and matted hair, and started down the avenue. We waved until she was out of sight.

It was quiet at the Pavilion once the refugees and their children were gone. The village women brought us schnapps and more seeds in exchange for vegetables and fruit, and sometimes they brought eggs and even a chicken, enabling us to start a henhouse of our own. There were mushrooms in the forest and watercress in the river. I made coffee from dandelions, putting the leaves to dry in the sun before baking the roots in the brick oven Bresla built in the yard. Madame Tkvarcheli taught me to make schnapps, using beech leaves and wild buckthorn. Many nights, we had mushroom soup, pickled walnuts, watercress, plums, raspberry tea, and schnapps for supper, and we found ourselves wondering why we hadn't eaten like that every night of our lives.

The Russians forbade the reading of any newspaper but their own, which was written in German and distributed weekly. We no longer had a wireless, but friends from neighboring villages, having learned of our survival, walked for miles to bring us news, and perhaps a gift of a sausage or three trembling doves gathered in a handkerchief, and we gave the visitors our own news and fruit from the orchard. The Russians had ordered the towns in their sector to close all bakeries, arranging for the distribution of small amounts of mealy flour so that women would be forced to make their own bread. I asked the baker's wife to teach me how to bake in exchange for fruit. I took to it very naturally, baking the bread in old garden pots. "It's your peasant blood," Kreck said, trying to swallow a piece of my first loaf.

I wrote again to my mother and father, reminded of them by Kreck's remark, which would have incensed my mother (I was going to tell her if I ever saw her again), to let them know that I was well. I wrote to Mr. Knox, enclosing a record I'd begun to keep of the birds I saw at Löwendorf, some of which had not been seen in years. I wondered if the birds had fled the war and only recently had felt it safe to return, but I didn't mention my theory to my old teacher. As there were no stamps and no one I could ask to carry them, I kept the two letters under my mat until I found a reliable courier.

Our new garden provided enough vegetables for our small household and for the women who helped us (levies of produce, grain, and meat were sent each month to the army, only now it was the Russian army). Every town and village had been required to accept a certain number of displaced persons, and Löwendorf had been told to take ninety of them. It would double the number of residents, and rooms and clothes and food had yet to be found for all of them. The country people were enraged to have to share their meager supplies with strangers who, they complained, did not even speak German. Every egg, every spoon of jam was begrudged the foreigners, who were viewed with mistrust and even revulsion, as it was conveniently said that they were to blame for the war. Even the Germans expelled from the Sudetenland were not spared the contempt of the villagers.

Frau Kronkeit, the widow of a farmer who'd been killed at Sevastopol, stopped me one day as I returned from a lesson in baking to complain that life had been far better under Hitler than under the Russians. She must have sensed my disgust, for she shouted after me, "*Nun bist du doch ebenso arm wie wir.*" Now, at last, you are as poor as we are.

The new mayor of Löwendorf, Herr Pflüger, sent word to Felix that as the schoolmaster was presumed dead, the village would be in need of a schoolteacher. As Herr Pflüger now had a say in the matter, he wished to discuss the appointment of the new master (the Metzenburgs traditionally paid the schoolmaster's salary and provided the schoolhouse with wood). I was in the room when the boy delivered the mayor's message—as there was no paper, the boy had memorized the words and recited them in a rush so as not to forget them.

I often wondered if my letters had reached Herr Elias (I liked to imagine him reading them). I regretted that I had no souvenirs of him—not my German dictionary or the Fontane novels or the tray cloth I'd made for him. That afternoon, I walked to his house in the village, but Russian soldiers were living there, and I turned around and walked home.

Later, as I worked with Dorothea in the garden—it was light until nine o'clock—I heard the song of a marsh warbler and stopped to listen to it, wondering dreamily if it had flown over the women on their long walk home to the Black Sea. Dorothea, who was watching me, said, "Don't sentimentalize things. Not now." When I asked what she meant, she said, "The marsh warbler imitates to perfection more than seventy-five birds. There's no knowing who he is tonight."

There is no knowing who *you* are, I thought. I had no idea that Dorothea knew about birds. I did not tell her about the soldiers living in Herr Elias's house.

As soon as Felix was strong enough, I walked with him to the village to apply for the certificate that would declare him a *Kleinbauer,* or small farmer. While waiting our turn, I noticed a man nervously explaining to Herr Pflüger his need for transit papers. Felix thought that the man must be a survivor of a camp because of his emaciation, as well as his expression of worn derangement, and he invited him to share our small lunch—Dorothea, fearful that the wait might be long in our newly socialist village, had given us buckthorn jam with a loaf of my gummy black bread. The man, whose name was Daniel Vrooman, was grateful for the food, and Felix told him that should he be unsuccessful in his efforts, he was welcome to stop at the Pavilion.

When Herr Pflüger caught sight of Felix among the supplicants, he beckoned him quickly into the small sitting room that served as his office. Still possessed of his unsettling combination of obsequy and contempt, he made me a mocking bow. "Comrade Palmer," he said.

To the accompaniment of Franz Lehar's "The Land of

Smiles," played rather too loud on a gramophone that looked familiar, Herr Pflüger told Felix that, as mayor, he would be more than delighted to oblige Felix with a classification of small farmer, in exchange for the orchard at Löwendorf, as well as the ruins of the Yellow Palace and the rest of the motorcars in the garage and, as an afterthought, the garage itself.

Felix and I walked to the Pavilion so that Felix could discuss Herr Pflüger's offer with Dorothea. As they had little choice, the Metzenburgs decided to give the mayor what he wanted. It was dangerous for them as owners of a large hereditary estate in a Communist zone. The resentment and envy that some of the villagers had felt long before the arrival of the Russians was now expressed openly, and the Metzenburgs had been denounced more than once as rich capitalists whose family fortune had been made through the sweat of the oppressed.

Felix and I returned to the village accompanied by Bessie, whom Felix held on a rope (the remaining two dogs had disappeared with the Russian tank). There were only a few lorries on the road, and it was very warm. Groups of German prisoners of war, guarded by American soldiers, walked past listlessly, and the Americans were startled when Felix greeted them in English.

The pleased, although hardly surprised, Herr Pflüger told Felix that he was very fortunate to have the mayor as his devoted friend, as there had been talk about the Metzenburgs. "In fact," confessed Herr Pflüger, "the Russians suggested that I exile you to another district, but now we can keep you and dear Frau Metzenburg with us. I'll tell them that you are properly registered as a small farmer, and that the produce from

your kitchen garden and your orchards goes directly to Berlin."
When we left, he gave Felix six packs of Camel cigarettes as a
consolation prize.

We walked home in silence, Felix holding Bessie's rope. The
dog didn't require a lead and would never run off, but he liked
to keep her close to him. "If we were ever in doubt," Felix said,
pausing to open one of the packs, "we now know for certain
that Rousseau was wrong."

In late July, a letter from Inéz was found in the stables. She
wrote that, after divorcing her Egyptian prince, she'd found
herself in London with her two children, where she had married an English group captain with a large estate near Bath. Her
new husband had recently been elected to Parliament, and she
pressed the Metzenburgs to come to stay with them.

Dorothea smiled as she read the letter a second time. "Do
you remember when she said that Christ was the only person
in history who combined an elegance of soul with an elegance
of both body and dress?"

"She has a genius for superficiality," said Felix. He'd been
reading aloud from a torn copy of Simenon's *The Hotel Majes-
tic*, holding the pages close to his face as his eyeglasses had
been stolen. I sat next to him as he read (his voice was weak).
His teeth pained him, and he packed them with melted candle
drippings, giving him a slight lisp. I couldn't bear to be away
from him for too long. I worried that he'd need me or, worse,
that I would need him.

There was a horse chestnut that grew behind the Pavilion,

and when the wind drew from the tree a humming noise, it frightened me. It was then that I reminded myself that tanks no longer rumbled through the park. Bombers no longer streaked overhead. In autumn, I knew, the paths would once again be slippery with leaves, and the brambles in the *Fasanerie*, once the covert of pheasant and partridge, would be heavy with fruit. In winter, I'd return wet and cold from my walk to the river. Bessie would race for the warmth of the fire, and I'd ask Kreck to save me some hot water. Felix would read aloud for an hour after dinner. I'd open the window in my room before I went to bed. I would drift lightly, as had become my habit, listening in my sleep should someone call me. Felix, perhaps, or Kreck. Or Caspar. Or Herr Elias. Or even the American.

One morning, I found Herr Vrooman, the man whom Felix and I met in the mayor's office, sitting at the gates, reading the Russian newspaper. I asked if I could help him. He rose stiffly and said in old German, his voice rising and falling in that pleasant way, that he hadn't liked to disturb Herr Metzenburg, not knowing his hours. He was hoping to see him after breakfast.

I suggested that he walk with me to the house. I knew that it was no longer acceptable to inquire of a person his place of origin or his destination, and I was silent as we walked up the avenue. I offered him a handful of cherries from my basket, which he accepted. Since the mayor had taken the orchard, I'd picked every cherry and plum that I could find, even if they were rotten, and my stomach had been swollen for days.

The avenue, once in near darkness thanks to the overhanging elms, was bright with light, and it was possible to see the river, shining at the bottom of the park, and the ruins of the Yellow Palace. The overgrown knot garden of thyme and barberry had gone to seed. The Russian soldiers had used the beds of white violets as a trash heap and the smell of rotting garbage drifted across the park, but the ash from the fire had fertilized the hundreds of elm seedlings growing in ranks along the drive and the heat of the fire had caused the spores and seeds of plants not seen at Löwendorf in years to burst into life. The outer walls of the Yellow Palace were covered with trailing Pelargonium, Ceterach ferns (which looked like bright green rickrack), and the lovely *Venushaarfarn*. Wild iris, hyacinth, and lilies grew among the fallen statues. The villagers, no longer in awe of the Metzenburgs, sometimes had picnics in the ruins, and small family parties. It was so lovely a spot that a stranger might be forgiven for thinking it a romantic folly, although I doubted if Herr Vrooman, looking at the ruins in curiosity, found them particularly sympathetic. Herr Pflüger, their new owner, had put up a sign, there and in the orchard, forbidding trespassers. An agitated jay followed us as far as the stable yard, mocking us with its laugh, and I was grateful for the distraction.

Felix did not come downstairs before noon, and I led Herr Vrooman to the library, where he sat in a broken chair to wait. I asked if he'd like a glass of water—it was already hot at nine in the morning—but he assured me that he was perfectly well. I felt that I should tend to him, but I could see that my attentions distressed him. I wondered if the close presence of other people was no longer tolerable to him. There was nothing I could say, nothing I could do for him, so I left him there.

Dorothea heard that the Americans and the English were buying, and she wished to dig up some of the treasure to sell in Berlin. Felix said that he'd prefer to hold on to things until prices were higher. There had been several messages from friends seeking the treasure they had entrusted to him, and he'd had to explain that the park had been destroyed and many of the objects entrusted to him stolen. He was hopeful that some of the treasure would be found, but it would take time. He wondered if his own beautiful things had survived and what their lives would be like with the end of the war. Dorothea knew that it was difficult for him to part with his treasure, whatever the price, and she promised that she would sell only those things that belonged to her.

She confided to me that she also hoped to inquire about friends in Berlin. It had become evident that people were no longer simply divided by class or race but by the different levels of suffering they had endured in the war. Those who had lost the most found it difficult to talk to or even to see those who had not suffered equally. It was not that they were incapable of sympathy, but that those who had suffered less than they had suffered did not awaken their curiosity or even their humor in the same way.

Dorothea asked me to go with her to Berlin, leaving Felix in the company of Herr Vrooman, who had moved into Roeder's old room. Over several weeks, Felix had learned that Herr

Vrooman was Belgian and a former professor at Ghent University, where his field of study had been fifteenth-century Gothic sculpture, particularly the work of Veit Stoss. In the fall of 1938, a few months before my own arrival in Berlin, Herr Vrooman, on his way to see the church of Casimir V in Kraków, had stopped in Berlin, where he was arrested the day after Kristallnacht. The SS had identified the buildings owned or occupied by Jews and arranged for the telephone wires, gas, and electricity to be cut, and there'd been no chance of escape. He and a cousin had been sent to Sachsenhausen prison, where his cousin had died. When the guards abandoned Sachsenhausen at the end of the war, Herr Vrooman managed to slip from the long line of prisoners. It took him a week to reach Löwendorf—he was headed for Kraków—where he collapsed in front of the inn, remaining there for two days until Madame Tkvarcheli found him and sent him to Herr Pflüger.

Although Herr Vrooman was too frail to help with the chores, he was an engaging companion for Felix. I often heard them talking, and I was relieved to see Felix slowly regain his spirits. When Felix told Herr Vrooman of the altarpieces, stained glass, and lime-wood figures that had been buried in the park, Herr Vrooman was speechless. When Felix told him that the carved wooden altar from St. Mary's Basilica in Kraków had been broken apart by the Nazis and taken to Nuremberg, Herr Vrooman burst into tears.

The day before we left for Berlin, Dorothea and I spent several hours in the park, Felix's treasure map in hand, trying to locate the spots where her jewelry was buried. Herr Vrooman offered to help, but Dorothea did not want to tax him with the effort of digging.

The park had been destroyed by the Russian tanks, and many of the trees cut for firewood, so Felix's map, drawn with such care, was more frustrating than helpful. Much of the treasure had been discovered by the soldiers, but after a morning of pacing and circling and probing and digging, we at last found a case of her jewelry and an iron trunk containing thirty medallions of mythological figures by James Tassie, although two Holbein paintings that had been buried with the medallions were gone. It had been very warm all week, and I found digging for emeralds far more tiring than digging for carrots.

Using strands of horsehair and my needle, I sewed the Empress Josephine's yellow diamonds, a handful of baroque pearls, five of the Tassie medallions (Adam Smith and Henry Raeburn, among others), and four gold watches that had belonged to Dorothea's father into the hems and seams of the clothes that we would wear to Berlin. Our dresses were much warmer than the weather required, but the weight of the treasure demanded fabric heavier than silk or linen. I felt a certain unaccustomed gaiety as we set out, as if we were taking a trip, which lasted until we reached the Ludwigsfelde train station.

A company of Russian infantry patrolled the station. Suddenly I could hear the heavy watches ticking noisily against my knees, and the clatter of fat pearls, rolling back and forth with every step. The train was meant for freight, and there were no seats or lights, which suited us, as we did not want to sit on the medallions. As we swayed back and forth with the hot and weary crowd, I thought of the Zoo flak tower and Herr Elias's lost books and the woman who had disappeared in a faint. As we drew near to Berlin (it was possible to judge distances and location by the extent of the destruction), a man standing next to me began to rub his face in my neck. I was certain that he could feel the jewels (I'd once feared that Herr Elias could hear the beating of my heart while we danced), and I twisted and turned, pushing his head from my shoulder. It seems he'd fallen asleep, and he apologized for the rest of the trip.

The train at last arrived in Berlin. The bridge leading to the station had been bombed, and there was no public transportation. People of all ages, their open hands thrust at us, hung on a sagging wire fence built to discourage the hungry from troubling those fortunate enough to ride a train. Dorothea gave them the food that we'd brought, and I had to stop her from giving away her hat, into which I had sewn two diamond rings.

We continued on foot, blinking in the light. The air was full of dust, and ash and soot soon covered our faces and clothes. The city was crowded with refugees. Cleaning brigades climbed over enormous piles of rubble. American military police directed traffic, mostly their own jeeps and lorries, and patrolled the streets, many of them blocked by fallen timber and brick. Some of the MPs were Negroes, and the children stood in silent rows to gape at them. Shelters had been built against the ruins with whatever materials could be scavenged, and women boiled vats of water over open fires.

We were shocked by the difference between the American and the Russian zones. Despite the endless destruction, the people, as well as the soldiers, were distinctly happier in the

American sector, and it made us envious. There was no electricity, running water, or gas, and little food, but there was a
mood of excitement, even elation, that made the ruined streets
and the faces of the survivors less desolate. I gave my collection
of letters to one of the smiling MPs to mail for me.

It took us some time to reach Dorothea's flat, and when we
at last found the square, empty of trees and houses, we realized
that we had walked past it more than once, confused by the
desolation. We walked to the shop of the dealer who Dorothea
had hoped would take her jewels, but the shop was empty. As
we walked to the Metzenburgs' bank, which meant entering
the Russian sector, we passed the street where Herr Kreutzer
had opened his last gallery. A man sweeping the street said
that drunken German soldiers had burned the building. He
didn't know anything about a Herr Kreutzer. When we at last
reached the bank, hot and thirsty, a Russian soldier at the door
shouted in German that the bank was now the property of
the Russian government. Dorothea sat on a pile of rocks and
began to cry. I sat next to her, the weighted hem of my dress
dragging in the dirt, until the soldier pointed his rifle at us and
ordered us to leave.

By the time that we found our way to the train station, it was
dark, and we were so tired and sad, our dresses so heavy with
unsold treasure, that we could barely walk.

After our trip to Berlin, Dorothea again considered the possibility of leaving the country. The Russians boasted that they
didn't take bribes, but it had quickly become evident that the

opposite was true. They were even greedier than the French, Dorothea said, and she was certain that she could obtain transit visas for us.

The natural envy of the local people had increased, in part because of the enforced classes in socialism that the Russians required us to attend each week in the schoolhouse. Dorothea and Felix dutifully took the seats saved for them in the front row out of a residual respect for their traditional position in the village, just as the first pew in the Presbyterian Church had always been left empty for them, even though they'd only appeared at Christmas and at Easter.

I often lay on my mat after supper, my legs swollen and sore, and listened to the Metzenburgs argue about leaving Löwendorf. The smell of my body was still strong, despite my frequent baths in the river, but Kreck and the Metzenburgs continued to pretend not to notice it.

Toward the end of August, a car came noisily up the avenue, gears shifting as it labored over the ruts. The car's headlights bounced across the bare walls of the room where we sat, before it came to a stop in the yard (even the sounds of Löwendorf were different—the paving had been stolen, and there was no longer the sound of hooves on cobbles). It was unusual for us to have visitors, particularly at night, but I wasn't alarmed. Kreck appeared in the hall, but Dorothea sent him away with a nod. She woke Felix, who'd fallen asleep in his chair. Bessie, who lay at his feet, stretched with a low whine and yawned.

Four men in suits followed a small man in a raincoat into

the room. It was immediately apparent that they were Russian because of their faces and their clothes, and because the small man didn't remove his hat. Herr Vrooman rose slowly from his chair, his book sliding from his lap. Felix, wearing new slippers I'd made for him, did not stand, and he did not ask the men to sit down.

The small man, scraping his muddy shoes on the rungs of a chair, informed Felix that he'd been denounced as an enemy of the Soviet Union. He apologized for intruding on such a *gemütliche* family scene, but it was necessary that Felix accompany the men to party headquarters. He was so courteous, so respectful, despite his hat, that it was obvious he was mocking him. "We have received a number of letters," he said. "You are known in Berlin to everyone."

"I confess I'm delighted to hear it," Felix said. "I thought most of my friends were dead."

The man, looking at the few broken pieces of furniture with unconcealed disappointment, said that Felix would be released in a few hours.

"Released?" Felix asked.

The man smiled. "You will be home in time for a good night's sleep." He closed his eyes and held his hands against the side of his face, pretending to sleep.

Felix put Herr Pflüger's cigarettes and a box of matches in his pocket. "I assume that it would be pointless to refuse?"

The man seemed to appreciate Felix's self-assured irritability. Not for the first time, I felt as if I were on a stage with actors playing their parts. As I watched them, I realized, somewhat belatedly, that I, too, was acting, although I could not be sure which part. I took Felix's arm, and he rested his hand atop mine for a moment, and then walked to the door.

The man in the hat turned to Herr Vrooman (he was only a supporting player and had not required his attention until Felix had said his lines) and nodded in a friendly way. Herr Vrooman, eyes bulging, nodded in return. The man then turned to Dorothea with an expression as if to say, You see how civilized we are, lady, despite what you think of us? Refusing to acknowledge him, she went to Felix.

"I regret that we only have need of your husband tonight, Frau Metzenburg," the man said with a smile.

Dorothea was stunned. "I'm not going? But of course I am."

Felix looked at me for a moment. Perhaps, I thought, this is what he had in mind that first morning in Berlin when he said that I might be of help to Dorothea one day. For an instant, I saw in his face his complete acceptance of life—it had always been there, but I had not understood until that moment. He kissed Dorothea and went into the yard, followed by the men. Halfway to the car, he turned back and said, "My book."

Dorothea asked him which book he wanted.

He smiled. "*Anna Karenina.* I haven't finished it."

She ran into the house and returned with the book he'd read many times, putting it in his hands as she kissed him again. Kreck stood with us in the yard. One of the Russians held open the door to the backseat, and Felix climbed inside. Two of the men squeezed next to him, one on either side.

We listened until we could no longer hear the car before we returned to the house. We sat in the front hall, the door open, too stunned to do more than trim the candle so that Felix would not return to a dark house. At dawn, Herr Vrooman rose stiffly, his hands shaking as he gripped the arms of his chair. I knew that if I tried to help him, he would wave me away in anger, and I watched in silence as he stumbled across the room.

I made dandelion coffee and brought a cup to Dorothea with a spoonful of jam, but she didn't want it. She moved a stool into the yard, where she would have a better view of the avenue. When I left to feed the chickens, she glanced at me for a moment but did not speak. When I returned, the stool was empty.

Kreck took the eggs from me. "Perhaps an omelet. Herr Felix likes an omelet with scallions," he said, and I went to pick some.

In the garden, Dorothea lay motionless on the ground, her face in the sand. I lifted her to her knees, and wiped her eyes and mouth. Together, we picked scallions, as well as some green tomatoes, and returned to the house.

Felix did not come home that night or the next or the night after that, although we were visited three days after his arrest by several Russian soldiers and two more men in suits. The soldiers searched the house, overturning in boredom the boxes that held our few belongings and idly kicking to pieces our last chairs.

I was alarmed to see that one of the men held Felix's keys in his hand. The man demanded that Dorothea tell them where the gold was hidden. When she said that there was no gold, he threw the keys at her. Herr Vrooman reached for them, but a soldier quickly picked them up and tossed them to the man.

We stood in the yard and watched in silence as they took what little remained in the house—two broken tables, some torn linen, a few plates and knives and forks—piling their loot into the back of the lorry that had followed them into the yard. I was relieved that they did not consider my small pile of books worth taking. Kreck dragged the straw garden chair that had been Dorothea's throne in the Night Wood into the yard, and she sat in it. She hadn't been in the chair five minutes before one of the soldiers nudged her shoulder with the tip of his gun and gestured that she was to get out of the chair. He threw the chair into the lorry, along with my bicycle.

"Where is my husband?" Dorothea asked each of the men, but they did not bother to answer her, busy watching one another to make sure that no one kept anything for himself, their contemptuous silence far more effective than any lie.

"When will Herr Metzenburg return?" Dorothea asked, following the men to the lorry.

"Perhaps next week," said one of the men, as if wary of accepting an invitation to dine. Her face brightened, and then he said, "Or we may return tomorrow. As we like. You'll have found your husband's papers and the gold by then." He grabbed her hand before she had time to pull it away, kissing her fingers with a loud smack. He tipped his hat, and they were gone, rattling down the avenue.

I'd hidden Bessie in the stables when I heard them coming up the avenue, and we went to find her. As Dorothea lifted the dog from the barrel, she noticed that the earth where the altar panels from the Church of Our Lady in Würzburg were buried had been disturbed. She fell to the ground and began to dig with her hands, Bessie joining her in excitement. I looked at Kreck, catching his eye for an instant before he turned away. The altar panels and two ivory crucifixes were gone.

"And Herr Vrooman?" Dorothea asked Kreck.

He nodded. Herr Vrooman was also gone.

That night, as Dorothea and I prepared for bed, I again told her that my name was Beatrice.

"Yes," she said, "why not a new name?" She paused. "Who shall I be?"

"It's not a new name," I said, but she wasn't listening.

Every morning and afternoon, we walked to the mayor's house in the village to inquire about Felix. And each time, Herr Pflüger said that he hadn't the slightest notion where Felix might be. He would not even concede that Felix had been taken away, although he did admit that if the men who came to the Pavilion were members of the Russian secret police, there was cause to be concerned. The villagers did not wish to be seen talking to us, in case local party members were watching, and they hurried away at the sight of us.

Dorothea slept on a mat in the hall so that she would hear Felix when he returned. Kreck fell into a lassitude so deep that he rarely spoke, and he no longer left his cot. I assumed his chores, as few as they were, and tended to the hens and to Bessie, as well as to the kitchen garden, preparing the food we'd grown ourselves and whatever I could find in the village. I wasn't strong enough yet to cut wood, and I found two boys in the village to help us (we discovered one morning that the wheelbarrow had been stolen).

Dorothea wrote letters to anyone who might be of help, although many of the men who once had influence were either dead or held in military prisons for war crimes. Friends of her father and Felix's friends in London and Madrid were hesitant and evasive, cautioning her to have patience. There was little they could do, especially as Löwendorf was under the authority of the Russians. Their own situations made it difficult for them to take much interest in the troubles of others. It's not that they were unkind, but that they had little of anything to spare.

It was the first time in twenty years that Dorothea had been apart from Felix. I found her going through a box that had escaped the notice of the Russians, with two of Felix's shirts, a hat, and the homemade razor. Dorothea held the hat to her face, hoping to find his smell. "It is just like him," she said excitedly, and pushed the hat into my hands, but all I could smell was wood smoke.

I went to the village every few days to barter vegetables, eggs, and herbs for milk, butter, and flour and to call on Caspar's mother. She had leased her field to Herr Pflüger, Caspar's man of the future, who had already put in a crop of wheat and rye. She hadn't seen Caspar, or had news of him, and like me, although we didn't say it, she feared that he was dead.

After years of war, the creatures that had lived in the house for generations—bats and mice and hedgehogs—once again took up residence. I listened at night to their scratching and rustling as they made themselves comfortable. I thought about the man in the Night Wood and I thought about Caspar. I thought about Herr Elias. Unlike Dorothea, I found no solace in the hope that Felix would return. I knew that the night that Felix climbed into the car, *Anna Karenina* under his arm, was the last time that I would see him. My sadness was not a heaviness but a weightlessness that frightened me.

Three weeks after Felix disappeared, as I carried water to the house, I felt such pain in my lower abdomen and in my back that I had to sit on the ground. I waited for the pain to ease—it came in sharp waves—and eventually I was able to crawl across the yard. As I neared the house, I felt a burst of warm liquid between my legs.

The milky shape of the child was barely visible in its cowl of blood and mucous. If I hadn't come across placentas in the fields, and seen the birth of foals and calves, I might not have understood. I'd been feeling unwell for several months, and my cycle was erratic. Because of my diet, the swelling in my body had been unremarkable—I'd thought that I'd begun to gain a little weight or else was bloated from the vegetables I'd been eating.

I looked around me. The women would not come to work in the garden until the late afternoon. Kreck and Dorothea were in the village, but I hadn't much time before they returned. My only witness was Bessie, who sniffed cautiously around me. She, like me, was shocked, but unlike me, she was curious. Pushing her aside, I scratched a shallow hole in the dirt. I did not want to touch it, and I used the hem of my skirt to push it into the hole. I packed the hole with dirt, tamping it down with my shoe, and dragged a rock from the pile next to the well to cover the little grave. That a child of the Russians had been growing inside me filled me with wonder. Never once did it occur to me that I had made it, too.

I crawled slowly to the house, pulling the excited dog after me. I made it as far as the back staircase before I had to stop, sitting at the foot of the stairs, my back against the wall. My bloody handprints were on the floor and walls, and there was a pool of blood at the kitchen door. I put Bessie in the laundry room, then pulled off my skirt and wiped the floor. I found a rag and folded it between my legs. I wiped the walls with a dish towel and hid the towel and my underpants and skirt behind a loose board. I pulled myself up the stairs, hand over hand, and lay on my side on the landing, rocking back and forth with pain. There was a little blood on the banister and I wiped it with my shirt—I knew that Kreck was nearly blind and wouldn't notice it, and Dorothea no longer came upstairs.

Later, when Kreck knocked on my door to ask if I would be having supper, I told him that I had a headache. He offered to bring me something. No, I said, I'm going to try to sleep. I listened to his soft shuffle as he slowly made his way downstairs.

For the first time in months, my body didn't smell.

. . .

A few days later, Dorothea told me that we were going to Berlin to look for Felix (at the mention of his name, Bessie lifted her head and looked around the room). She arranged for Bresla to move from her mother's house in the village to the Pavilion, where she would look after Kreck, who was too frail to be left on his own. An embarrassed Kreck, his burlap eye patch slipping from his eye, allowed us to carry him to Felix's old bedroom, where we made him as comfortable as possible on a fresh mattress of summer grass. Bresla would sleep in the dressing room nearby, with Bessie as her companion. There was enough food in the house and in the garden to last until the end of the year.

The night before we left Löwendorf, I made an opening in the sole of my shoe for Felix's torn and faded treasure map, which he'd slipped into my hand the night they took him away. I hid the map in the shoe and went to say good-bye to Kreck. He was asleep but awakened when he heard me at the door.

I sat on the floor alongside his mat and held his hand. Was it possible, I wondered, that we had never touched each other except by chance? Our fingers brushing as I handed him a cup. Our hands touching as we folded a blanket. I thought of the time six years earlier when I'd taken my father's hand, equally unfamiliar to me, and told him to think of my journey to Germany as an apprenticeship.

I thanked Kreck for all that he had done for me.

"Ah, yes," he said. "How to set a table and dust a chandelier. Very important in this new world. You can do that now, although I don't believe you ever intended to *clean* a chandelier. You'd rather sit under one."

I was pleased to see that he hadn't lost his malice. I wanted to go to bed (I was still bleeding), but I could see that he wished me to stay with him. "I was wondering," I said, "if you'd like me to trim your mustache." The white tips had grown into the hair at his temples and he looked like an old monkey. He said that he'd been waiting for me to ask. I used Caspar's hunting knife, given to me by his mother, and cut his mustache and then his hair.

"Mind you don't throw it away," he said, pointing to the hair I'd gathered into a pile.

"I wouldn't dream of it," I said.

"We can use it for something."

Dorothea learned that her father's villa in Dahlem, which had been given by the Nazis to the sculptor Arno Breker to use as his residence throughout the war, had not been destroyed, and we moved there in August. To our relief, the house was in the American zone. Herr Schumacher's lawyer, Herr Abbing, had survived the war, in large part because he was also Reichsmarschall Göring's lawyer. Fortunately he had the papers necessary to prove that Dorothea had inherited the house.

Dorothea left me to unpack our things, setting off at once for the nearby headquarters of the Americans. Only three rooms on the ground floor had not been damaged. All of the windows had been smashed, and broken glass, charred bricks, and pieces of plaster lay in piles in each of the rooms and on the terrace. There was one chair.

I decided that a torn tapestry could be used to cover the French doors at night, and the loose shutters would make good tables or even beds. As I cleaned the fireplace—books had been burned in it, as well as pictures—I remembered a photograph that had been in the library of the Yellow Palace. In the picture, entitled *Profondeurs du Sommeil,* a young woman in a skirt and sweater stretched comfortably across a narrow chimneypiece, her legs crossed at the ankle, her head resting in her palm, and I idly wondered if the mantel would hold me.

I'd brought some of my own much-improved brown bread and some salted fish given to us by Madame Tkvarcheli, as well as the cherries that Herr Pflüger had sent from his new orchard when he learned that we were going to Berlin. I hid our food and clothes and the treasure we'd been able to find at Löwendorf (Josephine's yellow diamond parure; a silver bowl by Cellini; the pearls; two Dürer goblets, the Hilliard miniature, two Houdon marble reliefs, one of them a dead thrush; some pewter, drawings, and silver; and several pieces of jewelry) behind a panel in the room that had once been the library.

I was bleeding, and I changed the rag in my underpants. I had cramps, and I stepped over the rubble on the terrace to rest on a stone bench that overlooked an enormous bronze sculpture of a man. The sun was hot on my bare legs and face and I felt happy. Before we left Löwendorf, I'd found a piece of broken mirror. I was surprised to see how much I had changed. I hadn't recognized myself. I was very thin. I'd lost quite a bit of hair. My eyelashes were gone, and my gums were bleeding, but I knew all that. What I hadn't known was that my teeth were gray, and my skin green. There were rings around my eyes. My eyes were yellow, the lids red and patchy. My nose curved to the side, and one of my nostrils was bigger than the other. Other than that, I didn't look too bad.

Over the years, I'd learned many things. I was less ignorant, of course, than when I arrived, a greedy girl from the west of Ireland. I'd known nothing of politics—I still knew nothing— taking my few opinions from Mr. Knox, who'd found it difficult to think beyond 1918. I knew that I was susceptible to influence—the high-minded Mr. Knox and his birds, Inéz and her finery, the Metzenburgs and their love of the past. I was easily impressed and easily gratified.

I understood that Inéz had once been Felix's mistress (and that when she said she'd lived with Felix as slave and master, it was Felix who had been the slave). I saw that the arrangements she had worked out for herself were not only profitable but also pleasurable, and that they had required discipline and even courage, as well as a deep cynicism.

I realized that the most charming man in Berlin, Count von Arnstadt, who was said to have died in Döberitz, had each week erased any incriminating conversations that he found on the Gestapo's secret telephone recordings before sending them to Hitler. The woman named Hilde Monte, whose illegal broadcasts Caspar and I heard on the radio and who bled to death when the SS at last caught her on the Swiss border, was the woman whose black feather hat I'd so admired at Christmas lunch. I understood that Kreck preferred men to women. I understood that Caspar loved me. And that I loved Herr Elias.

If the old world had remained the same, I would not have been invited to lunch with Felix at the Adlon, or to swim with Dorothea in the river, or to sit with them after dinner to listen to Jean Sablon sing "Two Sleepy People." Had the men not been sent to the war and the maids not been forced into slave labor, I would have disappeared into the sewing room with my bobbin and thread. I knew that the war had given me a life.

Dorothea returned soon after dark. She'd worried that the Americans and other buyers would not want the silver engraved with coronets and crests, but it was precisely what they wanted. It didn't matter if the initials didn't match their own. The monograms topped with crowns were better than their own initials.

"I saw the general's adjutant today," she said. "He was kind in that way Americans seem to be without any irony, and he promised to tell the general of Felix's disappearance. The Americans have made a devil's pact with the Russians. Herr Abbing told me in great bitterness that Field Marshall Montgomery was only days from Berlin when Churchill ordered him to hold back his army. I wonder what the English and the Americans have been promised in return for giving half of Berlin to Stalin."

I arranged our dinner on a piece of newspaper spread on the floor, but she didn't eat, even when I placed a piece of bread and some cherries in her hand. After I put away the food, we cleaned the corner where we planned to sleep, scratching in the dust like cats.

"As I described my plan to Herr Abbing, I noticed that he'd fallen asleep," she said as she moved a rag across the floor with her foot. "He wears dark glasses, so it took me a while to realize it, but then there was a snore that caused even Herr Abbing to jump. He's terrified that the Americans will arrest him."

I was silent, busy sweeping the corner with a piece of cardboard.

"Do you wish to go home?" she suddenly asked.

"We've only just arrived," I said in surprise.

"I ask because that, at least, could be arranged. Your mother and father may think you are dead."

I'd written twice to my mother and father since the end of the war, once when I returned from the Night Wood, but there was no way to know if they'd received my letters. I'd not had a letter from them, and they didn't have a telephone. I hadn't heard from Mr. Knox, either. "I can't imagine any other life—"

"Never could you have imagined *this* life," she said, interrupting me. "No one could have imagined it. I'm not sure even they imagined it."

"Felix said the same thing the day he took me to lunch at the Adlon. A girl flirted with him, and I was furious."

"That often happens. He's very attractive to women, as you know." She paused. "I sometimes wonder if you are in love with him."

I was silent, not because Dorothea was right, or because I didn't want to tell a lie, but because I didn't know the truth. "You and Felix have taught me everything I know."

"He always insists that it is *I* who have taught him." She paused. "Of course, it's true."

We talked through the night, mostly about Felix, and in the present tense. Near dawn, I heard her take some treasure from its hiding place and slip quietly from the house.

We'd eaten the last of our food by the end of the week, even though we were unable to eat more than a few bites at a time. There was food on the black market—meat and sugar and even real coffee, thanks to the Americans—but I was hesitant to leave the house. Dorothea was often gone all day. Her daily visits to anyone who might be able to help had given her hope that Felix would be found.

When I told her that I needed money for food—we needed water and soap as well—she said that there was none. She'd sold the last of the silver to Herr Witte, who'd given her a good price, considering that he'd sold many of the pieces to her mother, but she'd given all of the money to a lawyer recommended by Herr Abbing who claimed to be in touch with men who knew where Felix was being held and who, for a price, could arrange his release. When she returned to the lawyer's office, a furious clerk told her that the lawyer had gone abroad and had no plans to return to Berlin.

"But we have nothing to eat," I said, dismayed by her refusal to think of anything but Felix.

"There was a woman in his office who is also looking for her husband. He has the misfortune of bearing the same name as one of the commandants at Dachau. The Americans arrested him when the camp was liberated, and nothing will persuade them that he is not their man. Perhaps he *is* their man. She, too, gave the lawyer all of their money."

"I have the drawing that you gave me the night the Yellow Palace was bombed. Felix says it's a Veronese."

Dorothea looked surprised. "That belongs to you. Besides, there is more treasure at Löwendorf, although it won't be easy without his map."

I slid the map from its hiding place in my shoe and opened it. "There's nothing left," I said. She was standing at the garden door. The sky behind her was filled with light, and I couldn't see her face. "In the beginning, he only took a few things at a time, and never the best. He'd hidden so much. It was like Aladdin's cave. It was inconceivable that it would ever run out. There were so many people to help."

She slowly crossed the room to take the map from my hand.

"He used it for many things," I said. "Not just food. There were bribes. And documents. A ship, perhaps. There was much that I didn't know. I only discovered it at the end. He said that it was necessary to keep things from you in case you were arrested. He made me promise not to tell you. Until we went to the Night Wood, he awoke each day expecting them to take you away."

"I never understood why they didn't arrest us," she said. "Perhaps they thought we were too frivolous and foolish, although there were many like us who were shot in the street. I sometimes wondered if Felix gave them money, but, of course, no matter how much you gave them, they took you if they wanted you." The map was beginning to tear at the creases, and she folded it carefully. "The Cranach?" she asked.

I nodded. When all of it began, I'd never heard of Augsberg silver. Or Nymphenburg porcelain. Or Hans Memling. Or *oeufs en gelée*, for that matter. I looked at my hands, calloused and chapped, the fingernails broken and split. "I can still sew," I said. "There will be an interest in lace again. And what I have left of my savings. Nearly twenty pounds."

"Could you teach me to sew?" she asked.

I hesitated. "Your very own lace maker," I said.

"I've wanted to tell you for some time that I've never liked lace as much as I'm meant to like it." She began to laugh. "It was my father who loved lace and, like many things, it was just assumed that I loved it, too." She was laughing so hard that she began to choke.

"I never finished your dress," I said when she at last composed herself.

She wiped her eyes on her sleeve. "Too late now." She sat in the chair and slipped her feet from her shoes to rub her dirty toes.

"They say Inéz is a spy, but not for our side."

"Our side?" She smiled. "It wouldn't surprise me." She thought about it. "I never imagined that she was in Ireland for the hunting. At least not for foxes. Of course, she needed your Irish passport. Her position was always tenuous, despite her German marriage. There were rumors that she was born in Armenia, which counts for less than Cuba, I'm afraid, and that her papers were forged. Once she was Farouk's courier, she didn't need any of us. She didn't even need papers. Now she's Lady Averill. Any kindness one now receives from her ladyship will be disinterested. Perhaps."

I knew that Inéz was an adventuress without a conscience, but it had never occurred to me that she had used me for my papers. I wished that Felix had been there to share the joke, but then I realized that he must have known all along. I consoled myself with the thought that as much as Inéz had taken advantage of me, I had taken advantage of Inéz.

Dorothea continued to visit the headquarters of the Americans each morning, reasoning that if she made a pest of herself she might have a chance of getting their attention. The crooked lawyer's office was closed—even the angry clerk had fled. Dorothea saw those of Felix's old friends and colleagues who had survived, coming away astonished that they had returned so quickly to their former lives as great men of the nineteenth century, talking about ententes, embassy postings, restaurants, and women.

She gave me the money she received for the Dürer goblets, and I walked each day to the market run by the Americans and then to the black market. The relief that we felt to be under the protection of the Americans both soothed us and filled us with dread. It was temporary, we knew.

I brought home the newspaper of the American army, and I studied the mysterious cartoons and read the dispatches from

THE LIFE OF OBJECTS

the Pacific. I read the paper aloud to her each evening, and we discussed the liberation of the Philippines and the sinking of the *Indianapolis* until we were exhausted by emotion. We shared a pack of cigarettes a day, even though they made us sick. We consumed so much chocolate and tinned sardines and Nescafé with powdered milk that we sometimes spoke wistfully of our suppers of wild mushrooms and watercress. I bought a bolt of navy-blue silk and thread and needles on the black market to make us each a fall suit, and when I took our measurements, using my fingers as a guide, we were astonished at the weight we'd gained.

Our days had moments when we were lighthearted, and even girlish. There were no air raids. No sirens and searchlights. No fires or corpses. No arrests or executions. The war was over, and we, at least, were alive.

I liked to sit on the terrace each afternoon when the day had increased in warmth, in the hope that the sun would heal some of my more superficial ailments. One day, I saw a woman in a heavy coat standing next to the Breker sculpture of the man. When she did not leave, I walked across the dry grass and asked her into the house. I offered to take her coat, given the heat, but she shook her head. Dorothea, who was making a new list of American diplomats in Berlin, rose from her chair and insisted that the woman, who seemed ill, sit in it.

The hair at the woman's temples was dark with perspiration, and she found it difficult to look at us, snapping and unsnapping her worn handbag. I brought her a glass of water, and we waited patiently as she calmed herself, taking a big draft of air and holding it in her lungs before expelling it with a moan.

The woman, whose name was Frau Dremmler, was the wife of a doctor who'd been arrested by the Russians in May. He had refused throughout the war to join the Nazi Party, despite relentless pressure and threats. Most of his patients had dropped away in fear of the Gestapo, but he had continued to treat Jews, Communists, and even homosexuals. Against all logic, the Nazis had left him alone, their power maintained in part by the arbitrariness of their persecution. At the end of the war, the Russians, needing doctors for their many camps holding political prisoners, arrested him and sent him to Sachsenhausen, where they had recently replaced the Nazis as jailers. With her husband in the camp were Red Army deserters, Trotskyites, partisans from Eastern Europe, German officers, soldiers with venereal disease, White Russian officers and anyone else suspected of being an enemy of communism. A prisoner who'd recently been released had been asked by the doctor to tell his wife that he was alive. Once her husband had realized that the Russians had no intention of freeing him, the population of the camp increasing daily, he had abandoned all personal concerns and devoted himself to his fellow prisoners. One of whom was Felix Metzenburg.

Dorothea walked to the window.

Frau Dremmler paused. "Some of the prisoners are let go for no reason at all, and some are kept."

"And my husband?" Dorothea asked, her back to us.

The woman exhaled slowly and somewhat unwillingly. "Your husband was taken to Sachsenhausen the night of his arrest." She took a handkerchief from her bag and wiped her face. "He died of starvation ten days ago. He was buried by my husband at the edge of the camp, along with several other men."

Dorothea was silent. I asked Frau Dremmler if I could bring her another glass of water, but she waved her hand nervously. Now that she'd brought her news, she wanted to leave as quickly as possible. I saw that she could not bear much more sorrow, and I helped her to her feet—she was not old, but she moved as if she were crippled with age. She assured me that she knew her way home.

Dorothea was still at the window when I returned from seeing Frau Dremmler to the street. When she turned to me, I saw that her eyes were dry. "What would Felix do?" she asked.

To my surprise, Dieter was at the front door the next morning when I left the house. He'd gained weight, too, perhaps because he'd spent the last years of the war near the Danish border, hiding on his wife's family's dairy farm, where they'd survived on milk, cheese, meat, and butter, selling what they didn't eat for exorbitant prices on the black market. He'd been able to buy a small piece of land near his father-in-law's farm. "How nice," I said, mostly happy for him.

He had an artificial arm attached to his shoulder with a new leather strap. He'd finagled himself a job as guide to an American colonel whose military driver had yet to master the chaos of the city—there were no street signs, and many of the streets and squares had disappeared altogether. He smiled mysteriously and said that the colonel's driver was in his debt—Dieter was able to use the jeep whenever the colonel left the country, which was as often as twice a month.

I told him that Felix and Herr Elias were dead and that Caspar had disappeared. He pulled his American cap from his head and said that he was very sorry to hear it. I asked him to return in the morning, when perhaps Frau Metzenburg would see him.

He arrived with a loaf of sliced white bread, a jar of Nescafé, powdered eggs, and three bars of Palmolive soap from the American PX. I boiled coffee on a little stove I'd made with bricks and a piece of iron railing. Dorothea was in the garden. He asked about Löwendorf, and I told him of Herr Pflüger's success. He invited me to visit him in Schleswig-Holstein—he was only in Berlin long enough to earn the money he needed to buy some milk cows, his father-in-law's herd having been poisoned by their Danish neighbors as soon as the war ended.

As he was leaving, I took him into the garden, and he shook hands with Dorothea. I told her about the food, and she thanked him. We walked with him to the street, and I asked if he could use the colonel's jeep to drive to Rotterdam—I'd estimated that he could drive there and back in three days' time. He said that the colonel was scheduled to leave Berlin the following week for a meeting in Brussels, when he would be able to drive wherever he liked. Provided, of course, that the car was returned in time. Which rules out Shanghai, he said with a nervous laugh.

"I hadn't realized that you were thinking of traveling," Dorothea said when we returned to the house. She opened my passport, which I'd left on the windowsill. "You name really is Beatrice," she said in surprise.

"I'm hoping that you will come with me." I waited for her answer, but she was silent.

That night, she removed what was left of the treasure—Houdon's dead thrush, two diamond bracelets, the Hilliard miniature she'd given to Felix for his birthday, a goblet, two gold clips in the shape of question marks, and a sapphire brooch. "Do you think that Dieter would be happy with a brooch?" she asked.

I said that I thought he would be happy, and his wife very happy. As I wrapped the brooch in newspaper, she asked, "Will you go without me?"

I tied a piece of string around the package. "Yes," I said.

Word came at the end of the week from Madame Tkvarcheli that Kreck had succumbed without pain to his lingering afflictions, chief among them old age. Bresla was with him when he died.

Dorothea washed her face and combed her hair and went to her father's lawyer. Despite his disapproval (mainly because they were Russian, but also because of the old distinctions), she gave Madame Tkvarcheli the use of the Pavilion, kitchen garden, and stables for her lifetime, retaining the land, including the Night Wood. She arranged to send the women some money, with the understanding that she would send more. When I asked what would become of the Pavilion once Madame Tkvarcheli was dead, Dorothea said, "It goes to you, of course." At my look of surprise, she said, "I never want to see Löwendorf again, but you may."

I packed some food, although not my new suit, which I draped over the back of the chair to keep it from wrinkling. My shoes were in shreds, but there was nothing I could do about that. I rolled the Veronese very thin and sewed it into the hem of the jacket—there was a surfeit of art and jewelry in Berlin, and I was waiting until I reached Holland to sell it. I didn't have a plan, but the lack of one, or even a final destination, was appealing to me. Having grown accustomed to uncertainty, I was uneasy and suspicious without it.

Despite the many invitations that Dorothea had received— Inéz in Bath, friends in New York and Capetown, and Felix's sister in Buenos Aires—she said that she wasn't ready to see them. The Red Cross had forwarded a letter from my father to Herr Abbing, and he had given it to Dorothea that morning— he'd had it for a week, he said, but had forgotten it. My father wrote that Mr. Knox had spent a week that spring in Dublin at a gathering of ornithologists. Lady Vaughan's eldest son had been killed in North Africa. The byre where the Catholic girls used to sew had been struck by lightning. Business at the shop, now that the war was over and people could at last get on with their lives, was somewhat better. He wrote that he and my mother would be happy to see me should I ever find myself in Ireland.

I read the letter to Dorothea as she put on her suit. It looked well on her—on both of us—perhaps because we'd gained even more weight.

"It's a relief not to be expected," I said, and she smiled.

ACKNOWLEDGMENTS

I began to think about writing *The Life of Objects* in 2006, during my five months in Berlin as a fellow at the American Academy. Without the gift of that fellowship, I would not have read the hundreds of journals and memoirs written about the war, and in particular Lali Horstmann's *Nothing for Tears* and Hans-Georg von Studnitz's *While Berlin Burns*, that served to awaken my curiosity and, in time, to lead me to my story. I am indebted to Gary Smith for inviting me to the American Academy, and for his care and advice.

I began to write the book at the Ballinglen Arts Foundation in Ballycastle, Ireland, where I was grateful to have the friendship of Úna Forde, Christine Tighe, Brian and Sheila Polke, and Heather Bourke.

I wish to thank Sabine Russ in New York and Miranda Robbins and Françoise von Roy in Berlin for their fastidious reading of the manuscript, and their astute, subtle (and imaginative) attempts to keep me, as much as is possible, from error.

A NOTE ON THE TYPE

The text of this book was set in Giovanni, a typeface influenced by the classic proportions of Bembo and Garamond, and by Roman inscriptional capitals, but modeled to achieve a more contemporary graphic feel. Giovanni was introduced by the International Typeface Corporation in 1989.

Composed by North Market Street Graphics,
Lancaster, Pennsylvania

Printed and bound by Berryville Graphics,
Berryville, Virginia

Designed by Maggie Hinders